EXCELLER SELECT

TOP PICKS

WINGS *of* *a* DREAM

WINGS *of* *a* DREAM

ANTARA SARKAR

EXCELLER BOOKS®
A GLOBAL PRESS

Wings of a Dream

Cover by Exceller Books
Translated by Shuvra Dey (Tales Talks Walks)

ISBN: 978-93-47397-48-6

Published in India in 2025 by Exceller Books,

An imprint of GE Group,
G1, Dream Apartment, Degree College Road, Belgharia,
Kolkata, 700056, India
www.excellerbooks.com

EXCELLER BOOKS®
A GLOBAL PRESS

To my dear mother devoted to the welfare of others

Contents

Chapter 1

Srimoyee Sen worked in a renowned private school in South Kolkata. It had been almost eight years since she started her career at this school. During her early years at the academy, a South Indian woman joined the all-girls' institution as its principal. She was a very gentle, soft-spoken, and very friendly person. After five years, she opted for a transfer to a private school in Delhi and left Kolkata. Miss Sucheta Sanyal, the new principal, replaced her. Miss Sanyal was very different from her former colleague. A stickler for rules, she was strict and unyielding, controlling the school with an iron fist, leaving little room for dissent or individual freedom. No one dared to raise their voice in her presence. Everyone, including gatekeepers, watchmen and students, was in awe of her. Earlier, the staff room was a lively corner with the walls reverberating with laughter and shared stories that bounced off the high ceilings. The cacophony of joy seemed to banish all thoughts of lesson plans and deadlines. However, that familiar scenario changed soon after the new principal took charge. CCTV cameras were installed everywhere on the campus, including the teachers' staff room, which was now under constant surveillance.

Miss Sanyal's intimidating stance sent a shiver down anyone who approached her. Whenever she looked sternly through her glasses, even the smartest person felt weak. It had been eight years since Srimoyee had been teaching in this school. After clearing her B.Ed degree with flying colours, she did not have to waste time job hunting. The prestigious institution opened its gates wide and welcomed her with open arms. Like every year, the school planned to conduct an admission test for new students, and when the day finally arrived, Srimoyee was summoned to Principal Sucheta Sanyal's office during recess.

"Miss Sen, today we will be conducting an admission test for new kids, and you will have to supervise the interview session. You will accompany me. There will be an introductory session with the children first, followed by a meeting with the parents. I want to get the selection phase over as soon as possible today." Srimoyee beamed charmingly and nodded in consent.

In the last three years, since Miss Sanyal assumed responsibility for the school, she had transformed the academy into a centre of excellence by modernising infrastructure, adopting innovative teaching methods, focusing on students' holistic development, fostering strong community engagement, and providing continuous professional development for teachers. Principal Sucheta Sanyal was a tenacious, dynamic and upright person whose accomplishments were a testament to her competence. The school's consistently brilliant performances in the secondary and higher secondary exams had made it the most sought-after institution, and parents were eager to admit their wards to the school. Locals were accustomed to seeing anxious guardians form interminable queues outside the school every year, the night before admission forms were released.

After all, every parent genuinely believes that once a child takes the entrance exam and successfully crosses the admission hurdle, they are accepted, and their future is secured. The school's popularity had reached its peak, chiefly due to the austere lady principal's concentrated efforts. On the threshold of fifty, Miss Sanyal was so passionate about her profession that she had chosen to remain single and continued to devote her full efforts to take the institution to new heights of glory.

Miss Sanyal asked, "Is it okay with you? Will you have any problem if you take up the assignment?"

"No, Ma'am," Srimoyee replied politely.

Srimoyee went back to the staff room. She took out her mobile phone and called her mother and said, "Don't wait for me at lunchtime today. Please have your meal on time, as I will be returning home really late. Our school will be conducting an admission test for young children, and I have been assigned to supervise the session. This will be a lengthy affair, and by the time we wind up and call it a day, it will be late in the evening."

Her mother's concern was palpable as she spoke from the other end. "Oh, but I didn't even pack you a proper lunch today. What will you have?"

This is a universal maternal problem. No mother is content unless she is assured that her progeny is properly fed.

"Don't worry, Mom. There are many eateries in the vicinity right outside the school. I shall buy and have something from one of the shops."

"Please be careful and take care."

"Mom, please remember to take your medicine on time in the evening."

Srimoyee disconnected the phone. She had come to Kolkata with her mother and had settled in this city 15 years ago. She did her MSc and B.Ed from Calcutta University and then joined the school. After setting foot in the town, the mother-daughter duo rented a small apartment on Sukiya Street in North Kolkata, and since then, they had been leading a quiet and peaceful life.

Time moved at a snail's pace until school got over for the day. Srimoyee went to Miss Sanyal's office and sat down comfortably on a chair. The admission test was in progress. Srimoyee was friendly and easy-going with the children, chatting with them and regaling them with funny stories and snippets, while Principal Ma'am was busy interviewing the parents.

As the admission process was coming to a close, the Bihari security guard hollered, "Sagarseni Mukherjee." Srimoyee was startled to hear the name. The name was once precious to her and her sole privilege. Yes, there was a time when those who were very close to her used to call her Sagarseni lovingly.

As soon as the name was called, a beautiful girl, dressed in a pristine white frock, presented herself in front of Srimoyee. She resembled a gorgeous little fairy. Srimoyee asked her, "So, your name is Sagarseni? It's a beautiful name."

"I know. I am as gorgeous as the ocean, that's why my father named me Sagarseni."

"Who is your favourite parent, your father or your mother?"

"Mom is hardly at home. I never see her. I love my dad very much."

"What is your favourite food?"

"Chicken pizza. My dad can make it."

"Wow, that's wonderful. By the way, your frock is gorgeous. Can you tell me what the colour of your dress is?"

"White. Oh, Miss, you don't seem to know anything. How will you be my teacher if you don't know anything?"

The youngster's reply was amusing, and Srimoyee burst out laughing. She asked, "Do you like to play?"

"Yes, I can make a house with building blocks."

"Oh, really? That's wonderful. Can you see those colourful blocks on that table? Just go and check them out and show me how you make a house with them."

Sagarseni promptly went near the table, and in no time, she was engrossed playing with the blocks.

Principal Ma'am called the security guard and ordered, "Call the child's parents."

As soon as the door opened partly, a voice glided through. "May I come in, Ma'am?"

Srimoyee was startled to hear the voice. What had been enshrined in the depths of her psyche for so long seemed to spring to life suddenly, like a volcanic eruption with pyroclastic flows, lava flows, and *lahars* (mudflows) gushing out from deep within. Her well-concealed memories, emotions and trauma seemed to break through the darkness, erupting from a fissure vent all of a sudden. Her memories evoked a "curtain of fire" as she sat stuck to her chair, stunned. She was not prepared for this shock.

Srimoyee's mind raced back to a time long ago, a day when dark clouds hovered in the sky. The annual monsoon season was at its peak. It was the month of *Shravan*. Almost every morning, as soon as she opened her window, Srimoyee would be greeted by a squall cloud, ready to pour down at any moment. The surrounding land would be submerged, with water everywhere as far as she could see. Their home resembled a houseboat, floating on water. However, her reverie would be interrupted most often by a voice yelling from the distant green fields. "Sagarseni, come, let's get drenched in the rain. Do you want to pick up water lilies? Come with me. Don't be scared, I will be with you. Come."

After aeons, the person who was once closest to Srimoyee's heart stood right before her eyes. All these years of detachment seemed to evaporate in thin air in moments. Despite the vast chasm of time, it felt like yesterday. Srimoyee felt stiflingly uncomfortable despite the AC running at 22 degrees. It was just the beginning of April, and Kolkata was experiencing a milder prelude before the overwhelming onslaught of summer. Principal Ma'am was busy with her laptop. Srimoyee gathered herself and asked, "Ma'am, can I take a break now? I just want to step out for a while for some fresh air, and I will be back soon."

"What happened? You look very unwell. Why are you sweating so profusely? Of course, you've been sitting for three hours at a stretch, so maybe you are not feeling well. Should I send for a doctor?"

"No ma'am, I just want to go out for a while and stretch my limbs if you permit me."

"Yes, sure! Anyway, we are already done with all the interviews, and this kid was the last candidate we had. Since we are wrapping things up with the admission process, you go out and take a walk, but don't leave for the day without submitting the papers."

Srimoyee nodded and raised her eyes to the man standing before her, whom she had once known so well. He was staring at her, and their gaze met for a split second before she lowered her head. Srimoyee rushed out of the office, as she felt suffocated.

She walked and stood in the long, open, deserted patio. Dusk was setting in, and a cool, moisture-laden breeze swept her face. It had drizzled somewhere in the vicinity. She looked at the vast expanse of the green playground, which seemed to baffle her with questions. She was incapable of providing explanations, and her frailty expressed itself in a deluge of tears streaming down her cheeks. Despite years of concentrated efforts that Srimoyee made to sever her ties with her painful memories and bury her past for good, nothing seemed to have worked, and she was incessantly haunted by recollections of the time she had chosen to erase. She would immerse herself in her work to keep herself preoccupied and avoid the stabbing pain, but on that fateful day, her frayed nerves failed her when she saw him standing a few feet away from her. Her mind was bombarded with questions she wanted to throw at him and demand answers to. She wanted to scream and ask him, "What was my fault? Couldn't you, for once, try to find out where and why things went wrong?"

Chapter 2

Srimoyee felt a little better and refreshed after she went to the washroom and splashed her face with water. She realised it had been almost half an hour since she rushed out of the Principal's office in a dazed state. She tried to pull herself together and assumed that Principal Madam's room was empty by now. It had been a long day, and she felt she needed to tidy up before going back to the office. She took out a comb from her bag, untied her long braid, combed her hair and tied it loosely into a bun. Srimoyee was never particular about her appearance and did not bother about grooming and preening. It was a different matter that the creator had been magnanimous while designing her. She was naturally attractive and pretty, the epitome of beauty and perfection. Light-complexioned with a sharp, well-sculpted nose, eyes like a pair of restless doves, thin lips, and long, silky mane flowing down to her waist — she was truly a paragon of beauty.

Srimoyee knocked on the ornate wooden door of Principal Ma'am's office. Miss Sanyal was busy writing down something on a paper. Her table was strewn with papers. Seeing Srimoyee, she raised her eyes and said, "I hope you are feeling better now. Please submit the admission papers and move on. It's already late now, so hurry up and go home. If you want, my driver can drop you off."

Srimoyee had been observing Principal Ma'am from close quarters since she joined the school, and she had surmised that the stiff, temperamental exterior of this hardworking and committed lady concealed a soft heart. She was compassionate and full of empathy. Although Srimoyee was in awe of her, she respected her deeply and held her in high esteem.

"It is barely 7 pm now, and public transport is easily available. I shall take a bus and go home."

"Okay then, get going. Today you have stayed back for so long and done me a huge favour. Actually, I didn't want to hand over this responsibility to anyone other than a humane teacher like you. Not everyone can interact casually with children."

Srimoyee said, "It is a great privilege and a reason for my utmost joy if I can do anything, no matter how insignificant, for our school. I continuously learn from you and realise the amount of discipline, patience, effort, and commitment it takes to run an organisation so seamlessly."

Miss Sanyal did not like being heaped with praises. In fact, she often grew suspicious of people who were vocal about her efficiency or praised her for her commitment to her cause. Being aware of Miss Sanyal's aversion, Srimoyee bade goodbye with a smile and left for the day.

Srimoyee exited from the school gate and started walking. She decided not to wait for a bus but to book a cab. She looked inside her bag and took out her mobile phone to hire a taxi. Suddenly, she got distracted when she heard a familiar voice calling her from behind. She stopped on her track and froze.

The stranger proceeded towards her confidently and asked her, "Can I talk to you for a moment? I've been waiting for a long time."

As soon as she turned around, she saw Arpan Mukherjee standing there, facing her. He had not changed at all. Suddenly, she had a vision of the past and remembered that, during their adolescence, after every quarrel, she would stop talking to him for long periods. However, these tiffs would not affect him at all. After a fortnight or so, unfazed by rows, he would stealthily appear from behind her and whisper, "Can I talk to you?"

But times had changed. The naïveté of childhood had been replaced by a harsh, grey, unforgiving world where everyone seemed to have lost their way in a mysterious maze. Srimoyee was bewildered and could not understand what would happen in the next moment. She felt a shiver down her spine as bizarre reflections clouded her brain.

Chapter 3

Both Arpan Mukherjee and Srimoyee hailed from Saptadinga village in Burdwan district. They were classmates since childhood. They were the best of friends, and as they grew older, their friendship turned into love. During the early phase of their fling, everything went well, but soon the lovebirds became the talk of the town. In any small rural backdrop, it does not take long for such gossip to spread like wildfire.

One day, Srimoyee returned home from school earlier than usual and was surprised to see Arpan's mother at their house. She had dropped in without prior notice. Srimoyee remained incognito and overheard the entire conversation between Arpan's mother and her mother, Lolita. She was glued to the spot when she heard the bombshell drop. Suddenly, the dense, enveloping mist cleared, and she discovered that she was a foster child. She heard for the first time that she did not belong to the Sen family, and that Lolita was not her biological mother! Her very existence seemed to crumble down in an edifice. Srimoyee heard that soon after Lolita and her husband, Biswanath Sen, got married, doctors confirmed that she would never be able to conceive. The couple was quick to decide the next course of action and went for adoption. The Sens took her in from an orphanage in Darjeeling when Srimoyee was barely a month old. Lolita went to stay with her parents for the next six months to conceal the infant's origin and stop rumour-mongers from speculating about her. Since then, no one in the village has ever known or suspected that Srimoyee was an adopted child.

Arpan's mother had heard from a few of her friends living in Darjeeling that Srimoyee was an adoptee. She was determined to work on the information and leave no stone unturned to unearth the truth. With that single-minded purpose, she had barged in one quiet afternoon to confront Lolita at her home. She was well aware that Lolita would be alone and that it would be easy to exploit her vulnerability.

Srimoyee heard Arpan's mother, Shuvra Devi, telling her mother, "Let me be very clear at the outset. I will never let my son marry an orphan. I have come to warn you to do whatever it takes to keep your daughter away from Arpan. If you can't handle your daughter now, I promise I will spill the beans and let it be known to all and sundry in the village that Srimoyee is not your daughter and you adopted her from an orphanage. Once this information becomes public, your daughter will get to know it, and you will be solely responsible for the consequences that will follow. When your daughter will learn the truth, she will either leave you or commit suicide. But if you leave this village with your daughter for good, I promise you, my lips will be sealed forever, and not a soul in this village will ever get an inkling of this secret. You know everything about our lineage, our nobility, and I shall do everything to preserve this aristocracy. So, please talk to your daughter and explain everything and ask her to stay away from my son."

Lolita had lost her husband barely six months ago. Her husband, Bishwanath Babu, had passed away after a prolonged and ceaseless battle with lung cancer. Fearing that if this news became public, it would reach Srimoyee, who would be devastated and probably leave, a terrified Lolita promised to forbid Srimoyee from interacting with Arpan. She also promised to leave the village forever with her daughter and relocate to Kolkata once Srimoyee's exams were over.

Lolita stayed true to her commitment. After Srimoyee cleared her higher secondary examination from the village school, Lolita sold her family's landed property and ancestral home in the village and resettled in Kolkata with Srimoyee. Bishwanath Babu's old and trusted friend, Avinash Pal, assisted them in settling down in the city. He had a three-story house on Sukhiya Street, and he rented out a two-room flat on the ground floor of his mansion for Lolita and Srimoyee to begin life afresh. Srimoyee completed her studies and got a position in the school. It had been a long time since they arrived in the city as complete strangers with not a soul to call one's own. It had been a long time since then.

Srimoyee was jolted out of her reverie as Arpan's voice hit her. He asked, "Hey, what are you doing here, stranding in the middle of the street? Are you going to remain here eternally? Come on, there is a cafe nearby. Let's go and sit there for a while."

Srimoyee glanced at Arpan's car. He followed her movement and said, "Who are you looking for? I dropped my daughter off at home before I came. My flat is just two minutes from here."

"I can't go to that cafe. Everyone here knows me."

"Then get in the car. There's a Punjabi restaurant at the corner of the road. Let's hit that spot."

"What's the point of wasting time talking to me now? Our relations had ended a long time ago."

"Oh, so you are alleging I was the one solely responsible for the break-up? Don't you think you were also at fault for the split-up? You left the village with your mother abruptly, without leaving any trail behind. It was as if you had evaporated from the face of the earth. After I discovered that you were gone, I was devastated and searched for you everywhere like a man possessed. I went around the entire village and knocked on every door, seeking any information that anyone could provide about you. I asked my friends, but they were all in the dark like me. Why did you do this to me? I could have given you everything. You know I had everything: a house, a car, and a fortune to secure a loving, happy and prosperous life for both of us."

"Please don't stand here and feign concern, as all eyes are on us right now. I have to come here every day to work and earn my living."

"In that case, just hop in the car, and we'll go."

Arpan opened the car door and sat in the driver's seat. Srimoyee was aware that Arpan was a stubborn individual ever since she had known him. She quietly got into the car and settled in. Arpan started the car, and soon they reached the restaurant. Srimoyee felt a lot better after they entered the bistro. She had left her house early in the morning with a light breakfast and had a light meal in the afternoon. However, her hunger evaporated as her past reappeared before her. She felt devastated.

"What will you have?"

"Nothing."

"You can't come here and sit quietly without eating anything."

Arpan summoned the waiter and ordered two plates of tandoori roti and fried chicken. Then he removed his glasses casually and put them on the table. He let out a deep breath and said, "Why did you ruin my life like this?"

"What are you saying? I ruined your life? You have an abundance of riches, a happy and complete family and such a lovely daughter. How can you say that I had ruined you?"

"This is my present. This wasn't the case in the past. You had left by then. Just before my final exam started, you distanced yourself and started behaving erratically with me. You would be rude and treat me like dirt. I felt betrayed, and my exams went for a toss. Soon after the exams, you left without bothering to communicate with anyone in the village. Do you know how people in the village talk about you?"

"People are free to speak, and they can say a lot of things, but I am not interested in knowing."

"My mother also echoed the sentiments of locals and validated their belief. They all insisted you had an intimate affair with Palash Charan Dutta, the boy who was crazy about you and followed you everywhere. They also believed you had a baby with him and hence left the village stealthily in the darkness of night to avoid scandals and cover up that sin."

"Well, that's okay. You also believed it."

"Do you remember the last letter you penned before parting? You had written, 'Forget me and move on, I'll never come back because I love someone else.' Now explain, who wrote this letter?" Arpan demanded to know from Srimoyee.

"Yes, I wrote it because your mother ordered me to write it," she replied.

"What? I don't understand this puzzle."

Srimoyee was dismissive and said, "What's the point of bringing up these issues after so many years? You're happily married and have a family to take care of. So, continue living your life. There's no need to dig out skeletons anymore."

"I have the right to know and unravel the most baffling mystery of my life. Please tell me," requested Arpan.

"Where was your sense of propriety and demand for transparency when you got married?" Srimoyee retorted.

"I did it at my mother's insistence. Believe me, there is not an iota of love or respect in our marital relationship. I have only been carrying a huge burden of duties and responsibilities ever since I married. Let me share a vignette of this very society we live in. Educated and proactive women take up the cause of the fair sex and raise their voice against infringement of pertinent issues like liberty, equality, justice, and violence, and a section of society gravitates to support the cause. Angry voices rise against men, targeting them as perpetrators of all evils. Unfortunately, the same society looks the other way when men become victims. They are left in the lurch to navigate their way alone. Society never acknowledges or extends a helping hand when men are oppressed. Men are conditioned to keep a brave front even when going through the most difficult phase of life, and bury their distress in their hearts. However, if a woman schemes to put her husband or partner in trouble, she only needs to holler, 'I am being tortured', and in no time, the civilised society comes to her aid and points fingers at the man and brands him as the evil culprit.

"My wife tricked me into legally transferring all papers relating to my property, including the sprawling ancestral house in the village, into her name. She is an immoral woman who doesn't have any qualms about hosting lavish parties in the flat where alcohol flows like water and gambling is a daily ritual. She tormented my mother, made up and related false, vulgar tales about me to hurt her feelings. My mother found it difficult to endure her ceaseless torture. Finally, my wife packed her off to an old-age home. When I'm at home, I'm constantly bullied, abused, and yelled at. I don't even get to dine peacefully. My father was lucky that he died and did not have to endure the agony. I wish I too could die and get my liberty…"

"No! Please don't say such things again," an agitated Srimoyee put her hand over his mouth to stop him.

Arpan was upset and looked emotionally distressed. He was now determined to pour his heart out to Srimoyee. "You have no idea, Sri, the endless number of times I tried to intervene and stop my mother from being sent to the old-age home, but Pamela, my wife, blackmailed me, saying, 'If you utter a word or counter my decision, trust me, I'll finish the girl off.' I feel utterly worthless. I can't take this anymore. I spend all my time at home with my daughter and try to protect her from the agony, but I realise I fail miserably. I am a loser and can't take this anymore. I can't. I have offered to divorce her and release her from this unhappy marriage several times, but every time she has dismissed my proposal. And now she has set her eyes on the elegant mansion that my father built in Santiniketan. She wants that land and building at any cost, but I will guard that property till my last breath and won't let her get away with that estate. That mansion is part of my father's dream project. He had built that huge house to set up an old-age home. I am tired of defending myself against a barrage of insults and accusations. I often have an intense urge to commit suicide and get over this never-ending trauma. I don't want to live anymore. Our lives have become a living hell, a nightmare solely because of this one woman, and the worst part is that I have turned into a mere spectator who has no power to stand up and combat the culprit. I curse myself for all my inadequacies, and this weight sits heavily on my heart. I am at the end of my rope, and I know I have reached my breaking point. It is time for me to quit and end all agonies."

Srimoyee clutched Arpan's hand and said, "Calm down. Even though the situation is complicated at the moment, it will not always remain the same. Be patient, and your hard times will ease. You possibly don't know why we left Saptagram secretly without informing anyone. One day, as I returned home from school, I discovered your mother in our house. She was engrossed in talking with my mother. From their conversation that day, I learned that the mother I had known all my life was actually not my biological mother! I was a foster child brought from an orphanage. This information shook my very foundation. The rug was suddenly pulled out from under me, and everything fell apart. I remained glued to my spot, speechless.

"I don't know who bore me, but I don't dare to deny the right of the mother who rescued me from an orphanage, accepted me and took me in her arms unconditionally, raised me with love and compassion all my life, rather than thinking about the one who disowned me at birth. I haven't ever spoken about it until today, nor have I sought any explanation from my mother, because I know if she realises that I know the truth, she will be deeply hurt and break down. So, when your mother said she wouldn't accept this relationship and threatened to make the information public if my mother continued to stay in the village with me, my mother was frightened and promised to leave the village and relocate somewhere far away. At this juncture, I was compelled to write you that letter and sever ties with you. Later, I reflected on it and realised I had taken the right decision. I was an orphan with no information about my lineage, my background. Hence, there was no point in getting involved in your life. So, I backed off. This would be mutually beneficial for us. Of course, your mother offered a hefty price in lieu, but my mother refused it. My mother sold our house and the land we had even before my exams were over. The day I took my last exam, we left the village at the crack of dawn and headed for Kolkata. We boarded the train to Howrah station and then headed to my father's friend's house. We stayed at his home and continued my studies. After completing my studies, I found a job at this school, and we gained financial stability; thus, life became easier. Now I teach students at home in my spare time."

"So much had been happening, and you did not tell me anything. My mother ruined my life like this? And you walked away from my life for my well-being? Do you think anything positive happened to me? Anyway, it's been many years since then, and one can't live one's entire life alone. Forget about whatever happened to me; you should get married now. Today, after so many years, I bumped into you so abruptly. Fate has been playing such bizarre games with us all our lives, and now we run into each other under the most peculiar of situations."

"I still remember the day you told me what was on your mind. I couldn't sleep all night with joy," Srimoyee recollected fondly.

"If I hadn't told you, you wouldn't have ever realised. God, how hard I had tried before to convey my feelings and convince you," Arpan reminisced.

"I understood everything, but I waited patiently because I wanted to hear it from you. Anyway, let's drop this topic here and move on. We both left that life far behind, buried the past, and nothing remains except a vast, impenetrable chasm."

"That's why I'm asking you to get married and settle down."

"I will. My wedding has been fixed with our landlord's son. Everything has been finalised except the date, which is likely to be resolved soon."

Srimoyee looked at Arpan and said to herself, "Don't you know I have been married to you since I was a child? You have my heart and mean the world to me. I regard you not just as my lover but my soulmate, my husband. The rest is nothing but a mere performative act, a charade, a fleeting moment like a fist of slipping sand that I hold in broad daylight. You occupy my heart, and there's no space for anyone else, even now, after so many years. However, our landlord has been kind and supportive throughout and helped us set up home and stabilise when we landed in this city, so when he came to my mother with the wedding proposal for his son with me, my mother agreed readily. You are already married, even though you are going through a difficult situation. I have no right to demand your attention.

The waiter came with the food and served it.

Arpan asked, "How is Auntie?"

"Mother hasn't been keeping very well of late. It's the usual tale with advancing age."

"I'll go and meet her one day."

Srimoyee finished her meal, and while wiping her face, she suddenly chanced upon Arpan looking at her attentively, without batting an eyelid.

"What are you looking at?" she asked.

"You have become even more beautiful and charming."

Srimoyee burst out laughing. She said, "Yes, and you have grown old, donning thick glasses and a salt-and-pepper beard for better effect!"

Arpan laughed.

"Where do you live now, and where do you work? Tell me about your journey. After completing your studies, how did you choose your path and reach this far? I don't know anything. Please enlighten me."

By this time, Srimoyee had regained her composure and felt much better. She felt a sense of joy, realising that the person she had loved all her life had also loved her, and that years of separation had not diminished that allure. Although she had left Arpan in the dark for decades, he had not given up on her, and she was the reigning queen of his heart. He had cherished her all along, and that was reason enough for Srimoyee to feel a deep sense of fulfilment. She breathed a sigh of relief.

Arpan suddenly said, "Promise me one thing: you will never break our friendship."

"I can't promise you this because the diktats of reality are very harsh and far removed from idealism. You're already married. What if the person I'm going to marry doesn't approve of me having a relationship with you? Besides, you can't deny that you spurned me that day in fierce hesitation and disbelief. However, today I feel at peace after I get to know that you actually looked for me after we had left Saptagram."

"I was quite young and immature in those days. I also went abroad for higher studies. After I returned, I joined a multinational company in Kolkata in a senior position. Soon enough, my parents were after my life and insisted I get married. My father passed away within a short period, and my daughter was born. This was the beginning of a downward spiral for the family. My wife became eccentric, volatile, whimsical, abusive and tyrannical. Anarchy reigned at home."

"Well, let bygones be bygones and make peace with the present. It's better to let go of the attachment to the past. You have to live in the present. Now you know everything you needed to know about me, and it is time for me to take my leave and flake off. Thank you for the treat today," Srimoyee was all set to leave.

"Thank you? Are you thanking me?" Arpan looked at her incredulously.

"Okay, I am sorry I hurt you. I'm withdrawing it."

"Come, I'll drop you home."

"You will not be there to drop me off at my house every day. What's the point in disrupting my routine and unsettling my regular pattern? Besides, tongues will wag, and neighbours will begin speculating if they see me getting out of a stranger's car."

"At least share your mobile number or WhatsApp before you go," Arpan pleaded.

"No, there's no need to do that because we are both weak and vulnerable, and this will only make things worse. Our paths have diverged, and the trail has separated into two distinct routes; our journey should also be different."

Saying this, Srimoyee walked out of the restaurant. She did not look back to see Arpan standing there, shocked.

Chapter 4

It had been a month since the admission tests were conducted, and now it was time to announce the names of the successful candidates who had cleared the interview hurdle. Guardians waited with bated breath outside the school gate, running their eyes over the list to see if their wards had been admitted to the elite school. Srimoyee was burning with curiosity to cross-check if Arpan had been honest with her. She had lost all faith in men, and despite Arpan being her former friend, she was still not sure whether he had told her the truth about his wife. She was on edge, obsessed with discovering the truth. She realised Arpan was in dire straits if what he said was true, and his life was in a real mess.

Srimoyee felt that if Sagarseni were accepted into the school, she would have the opportunity to speak to her. Although she was a teacher in the secondary section and would not be able to take classes in the primary section, if Sagarseni joined the school, she was sure to meet her at some point and talk to her. But then she reprimanded herself for being so inquisitive about Arpan and being so eager to verify his words. In a couple of days, she herself would be led to the gallows to be sacrificed on the altar of gratitude.

Srimoyee made her way through the large crowd of anxious guardians, all trying to reach the notice board outside the school and check the list to see if their children had made it. Srimoyee ran her eyes down the list and saw Sagarseni Mukherjee's name. Although Srimoyee had interviewed Sagarseni, Principal Ma'am was in charge, and she had finalised the list of successful candidates.

The school's new session commenced with the cacophony of fresh students, entering hurriedly. The campus looked like a garden bursting with fresh, bright flowers. One day, Srimoyee chanced upon Sagarseni sitting alone in a corner of the playground while her classmates played in gay abandon. It was lunch break. Srimoyee approached Sagarseni and asked, "Everyone is playing, why aren't you joining them? You are sitting alone. Have you had your lunch? What do you like to eat?"

The girl stood still with a gloomy face and remained quiet.

"You haven't eaten, right? But why?"

"Father was not feeling well today, and I don't feel like eating the food that Ganga auntie made for me."

"Where is your mother? Who is Ganga?"

"When I get ready for school, my mother closes her bedroom door and sleeps. I don't go to her room anymore. One day, I knocked on her door, and she was furious for waking her up and beat me up. Ganga auntie lives with us and does all the household chores. Every morning, she prepares me for school. Sometimes, Dad also prepares me for school."

Srimoyee was concerned, and she asked anxiously, "Didn't your dad prepare you for school today?"

"Father is running a temperature; his body is burning, and he hasn't been able to get up since morning. What will happen? Ganga auntie forced me to come to school. There's no one at home. There's no one to look after my father," Sagarseni sounded very upset.

"Can you run and get your school diary from your class now, please?"

As soon as Srimoyee said this, Sagarseni rushed to fetch her diary from the classroom and handed it to her. Srimoyee had packed poha in her lunch box. She called Sagarseni and offered her the food, saying, "You can try my meal."

Sagarseni was ravenous. She was excited to see the new food, and promptly took a spoonful from the box and put it in her mouth. She was delighted and exclaimed, "Wow, this is delicious! How do you make it? Can you please teach the recipe to Ganga auntie? She doesn't know how to cook at all."

Srimoyee was highly amused to hear Sagarseni's criticism of her Ganga auntie and burst out laughing.

After all these years, Srimoyee arrived home from school and sat at the dressing table. She took off her oxidised danglers from her ears and looked at herself critically in the mirror. She thought to herself that Arpan still considered her beautiful and felt that he had not lied. No, he did not lie, not even about his own wife, because children are innocent. They do not know deceit and hypocrisy. When a mother who does not bother to take care of her cute little daughter, her own progeny, how can she be expected to look after her husband? Srimoyee had saved Arpan's number on her mobile phone from Sagarseni's diary. She was now having an insane urge to call Arpan! She fiddled with her mobile, staring at Arpan's phone number, and resisted making the call. Her logical mind warned her of the consequences of taking a wrong step, reminding her that Arpan was already married. If she reconnected with him, society would not be kind to her. She would be branded as the 'other woman,' a 'homewrecker,' an immoral person, responsible for breaking a marriage. She would face social stigma and isolation. She knew even her mother, Lolita, had a very clear-cut opinion on this. Every other evening, while watching daily soaps on television, her mother often remarked indignantly about women who were shown to fall in love with married men. She would categorically blame women for getting involved in extramarital affairs and being the main reason for frequent divorces in middle-class homes.

But emotions often win over logic, and the mind finds its own way to disregard logic. Srimoyee's mind convinced her that Arpan was her childhood friend, her confidante, and he was unwell, so she had to call him. No other relationship could be an obstacle in this case. She dialled his number.

Arpan's phone rang. He took the call after some time. "Who is calling?" he asked.

His voice sounded husky. *He must have been sleeping* – Srimoyee thought to herself.

"Who is this calling? Please speak."

"It's me, Srimoyee."

"Oh, really? Is that you, Sri? Did you hear that I am going to die soon, and that's why you called me? It was by sheer chance that we met for the last time."

"What nonsense are you talking about?"

"I have a high fever, Sri. I can't talk. I can't even breathe."

"Why don't you call a doctor?" Srimoyee asked.

"No, there's no need. I don't want to live anymore. I have lost my will to continue like this. I just want to quit."

"I'm sending for a doctor. You'll be fine," Srimoyee insisted.

"No, don't bother. There's no need for all that. Just leave it," Arpan sounded miserable as he spoke with difficulty.

"Shut up and listen to what I say," Srimoyee reprimanded Arpan.

Srimoyee hung up the phone and called Dr Rajaditya Basu, a renowned cardiologist who had his chamber in South Kolkata. Srimoyee had been to his chamber many times with her mother for consultation. Dr Basu was an elderly gentleman well into his 60s. He was very fond of Srimoyee, not only because he had been treating Lolita for many years, but also because Srimoyee reminded him of his teenage niece, whom he had raised from childhood and lost in a freak road accident when she was just 14. There was another reason why Dr Basu doted on Srimoyee.

Once, while attending her colleague's reception party, Srimoyee was introduced to Dr Basu. On her way back from the party, Srimoyee's cab came to a screeching halt because two vehicles had collided ahead of them, and the road ahead was closed. When Srimoyee got out of the taxi, she was aghast to discover it was Dr Basu's car that was hit, and both the driver and Dr Basu lay unconscious in the car. The driver was bleeding profusely. Srimoyee immediately sought her cab driver's help, and together they rushed to a nearby hospital with the injured. She stayed at the hospital, and when both of them were released after treatment, she accompanied them to drop them off at home. Dr Basu was extremely moved, and her action further endeared her. He would often say that Srimoyee resembled his brother's deceased daughter.

Srimoyee called Dr Basu. "Hello, *Kakababu* (uncle)! I'm Srimoyee speaking. A friend of mine has suddenly fallen very ill. He has a high fever and shortness of breath. It is not possible to take him to the hospital now. So, could you please take a look at him and ascertain his condition?"

"Where does your friend live? It's already quite late in the evening, and my driver has to go home," Dr Basu said.

"Uncle, he lives very close to your chamber in Ballygunge. His flat is near my school."

"Alright. Send me his address on WhatsApp."

The sexagenarian physician treated his patients in his chamber and avoided attending in-home visits. However, he could not disregard Srimoyee's request. As soon as she sent him the address, Dr Basu left his chamber and reached Arpan's flat.

Ganga opened the door as soon as the doorbell rang, and Dr Basu entered. He went to Arpan's bedside and conducted a thorough examination. He then called up Srimoyee and said, "*Didibhai* (that's how he addressed her affectionately), your friend's condition is quite grave. He is frequently losing consciousness and gasping for breath. He needs to be hospitalised immediately. If you agree, I can admit him to my nursing home."

"Okay, *Kakababu*. It's quite late, and I can't do anything from here right now. Could you please do the needful so that he can be transported to your hospital at the earliest and you can initiate his treatment?"

"Okay. I am calling Shyamal, the ambulance driver at my nursing home. He is a dependable man, and he will take your friend safely to the nursing home."

"Okay. Please do whatever you think is required to stabilise him. Please, *Kakababu,* save him and don't worry about the expenses. Whatever the costs, I will pay for them."

"There, there, you go. If you say that again, *Didibhai,* I will be furious. Meanwhile, we have to complete some legal formalities before I can admit him. Any member of his family must sign the consent form before treatment commences. Since you are not related to him, you cannot admit a critical patient based on being his friend."

"He is married, but I don't know anything about his wife's whereabouts," Srimoyee informed.

"Yes, I know. When I asked the attendant, she informed me that his wife had been out of the station for the past three days," Dr Basu said.

"His mother is alive, but she lives far away. Can't we call her on the phone and seek her consent?" Srimoyee asked.

"Yes, that can be done, especially in case of an emergency. If the housekeeper has his mother's phone number, I'll take it from her and call her."

"Okay. Thank you so much, *Kakababu*. I'll be right over to your nursing home," Srimoyee sounded somewhat relieved.

With Ganga's help, Dr Basu called Arpan's mother for consent, following which Arpan was admitted to the nursing home that very night. Srimoyee took a taxi and headed straight to Dr Basu's nursing home.

Dr Basu was in his chamber. Srimoyee entered hurriedly and asked, "How is he now? What did you find, *Kakababu*?"

"Nothing can be said just now. I need to observe him for the next 24 hours before deciding on a course of action. I have administered an injection. He is sleeping now. He was having trouble breathing, so I put him on oxygen support. From the preliminary investigation, it seems he was neglecting his body. Don't go to his cabin now because he won't be able to talk."

"Please, *Kakababu,* I won't go near his bed. I will watch him from afar and come back soon. Can I go, please?" Srimoyee pleaded.

Dr Basu relented and permitted, saying, "Okay, go."

Srimoyee went to Arpan's cabin. She watched him from a distance and burst into tears. She said to herself, "The last time we met, I didn't believe a single word when he told me what he was going through. I can't think of anyone else in my life except him, but societal constraints stifle our journey together. Every time his thoughts peep into my mind, my conscience reminds me that he is married to another woman, and I can't have any rights over him or any expectations from him anymore. After we left our village and arrived in Kolkata, my father's friend provided us with rock-solid support. He sheltered us in his house. I have a roof over my head because of his magnanimity. How can I disregard him or his family when they seek something from me?"

Chapter 5

As usual, Srimoyee woke up at the crack of dawn. It was 4am. Her day's routine would begin on a hectic note as she rushed to the kitchen to cook breakfast and lunch, pack her snack, and leave for school. Her mother waited for her return in the afternoon, and then mother and daughter would have lunch together, chatting and taking stock of the day's events.

After Srimoyee returned from the hospital late at night, she went to bed but lay awake the entire night, sick with worries and could not sleep a wink. She waited impatiently for daybreak. With the first rays of the sun seeping in through her window, she sprang to her feet. She cooked breakfast for her mother, prepared vegetable soup for Arpan, and quickly got dressed up, all set to go to the nursing home. She had taken a day off from school, so she decided to return home after visiting Arpan and then cook lunch.

She had given her mother a hint about how she bumped into Arpan out of the blue, and also informed her that he was critically ill and was hospitalised. Lolita was at her wits' end when she heard the news. She warned Srimoyee, saying, "Don't forget that Arpan is a married man. Don't visit him frequently. You are going to get married to Bijon soon. So, stop worrying about useless stuff, and focus on your forthcoming wedding."

Bijon Pal was the son of Srimoyee's deceased father's friend, who was also their landlord. Bijon had completed his B.Com from a reputed college in Kolkata, and after completing a management course, had started his venture in Bengaluru. His company was doing very well, and he was striking it rich there. He often travelled abroad to meet his overseas clients and expand his business. Only the previous night had he returned home from Dubai after a month-long business trip.

When he noticed Srimoyee leaving home hurriedly so early in the morning, he offhandedly asked, "It looks like you have taken the day off from school. Are you going out somewhere? In fact, it's good that you took a day off. Only last night, my mother was saying, since the wedding is barely two months away, we have to get the shopping done before that."

"A childhood friend of mine has been hospitalised in a critical condition. I'm going there now and don't know when I'll be back," replied Srimoyee.

"I honour and value a woman's freedom, but don't forget that we are going to commit to a relationship soon. So, I expect that regard and time from you," Bijon insisted.

"That's right, but I don't have time right now." Saying this, Srimoyee hurriedly bypassed Bijon and left. She had decided to drop in at Arpan's flat before heading to the nursing home.

Srimoyee entered the posh nursing home. She took the elevator to the third floor and arrived at Dr Basu's chamber on the left side of the long, gleaming corridor.

"Good morning, *Kakababu*. How is my friend now? What is your assessment of the patient's condition?" Srimoyee sounded worried.

"Oh, he's improved a lot and is much better now. He is responding to treatment. I'm glad you called me at the right time yesterday. Things could have taken a grave turn if you hadn't got in touch with me then."

"Thank you very much, *Kakababu,* for answering my distress call and taking the initiative to rush to my friend's flat when it was already very late at night. You assessed his state and got him hospitalised. I can't imagine the consequences if you were not there," a grateful Srimoyee replied.

"Listen, we have to take a professional oath when we pass out of medical college. We promise that if required, we will try to save the patient at the cost of our own life, no matter what," Dr Basu replied.

"That's the reason we look up to doctors like you as God."

"I have scheduled several pathological tests on your friend today. I'll inform you when the reports come. He's no longer on oxygen support, so you can go and meet him now," Dr Basu said.

Arpan opened his eyes as daylight filtered through the white curtains and fell all over him. A young nurse stood in front of him, holding a thermometer.

"Good morning, Sir. How do you feel now? I need to check your fever."

The day before, Arpan was in a daze. But as day broke, he felt much better. The weight on his head had eased a lot. "Well, Sister, could you please tell me how I got in here?" he asked.

"I am sorry, Sir, I was on leave yesterday, so I'm afraid I do not have any information on this."

While the conversation was on, Srimoyee pushed open the heavy, dark glass door and entered the cabin. She looked at Arpan and asked, "How are you feeling now? Whatever information you seek, you can ask me."

"I know you did a lot for me yesterday. How can I thank you!" Arpan said.

"So, you're going to belittle me like this now?" Srimoyee asked sharply.

"No, no, you are misunderstanding me," Arpan clarified.

"Then all this talk is meaningless now. You have to get well first. You have a young daughter waiting anxiously for you. How are you feeling today?" Srimoyee asked Arpan and then turned to face the nurse and asked, "Does he still have a fever, sister?"

"Yes, madam, he is still running a temperature, but it has come down considerably," the nurse informed politely.

"Okay, thank you. You may go now. I will be around now for some time and will call you when I leave."

The nurse followed Srimoyee's instruction and briskly left the room.

Srimoyee took a container of piping-hot soup she had made at home out of her bag and placed it in front of Arpan.

"The soup is still quite hot. Just have it quietly," saying this, Srimoyee rummaged her bag and took out a towel and wrapped it around Arpan's chest.

"Why did you take so much trouble and bring this? The nursing home will anyway arrange my meals."

"I know, but I couldn't be at peace with myself. So, I consulted with *Kakababu* on what you should eat and then made this soup for you. Don't say a word, just have it quietly," Srimoyee insisted.

"I am feeling embarrassed. I have never been able to do anything for you. And, now, in a matter of days, you will be married, and I will not be able to do anything for you."

"The bond of friendship is unrivalled by any other tie. It is the most cherished and valuable of all relationships. We have been friends since infancy, we are still friends, and will be friends forever." Srimoyee reassured Arpan.

"That's not true or reasonable, Srimoyee, you know that, don't you? I was swayed by emotions and expressed whatever came to my mind that day, but there can't be such a thing as just friendship between us," Arpan said.

"Okay, you get well first, and then we can think it over and discuss. Please hold the spoon properly."

"I can't. My hands are trembling."

"Okay, don't worry. I will feed you."

"My little one will probably miss going to school today," Arpan sounded anxious.

"I knew you'd be worried. So, I got up early this morning and went to your flat. Ganga and I fed your daughter, packed her bag and sent her to school with her lunch pack. Don't worry about her. She'll be fine. As long as you are here, I will keep in touch with Sagarseni. I won't need to visit your flat daily, as I have trained Ganga today, and she will be able to handle everything independently."

"I feel so much at ease now," Arpan heaved a sigh of relief.

After Srimoyee finished feeding Arpan, she said, "I now plan to go and visit Dr Basu in his office and have a word with him about your progress. I took a day off today, but now that I see you are doing fine, I am thinking of cancelling the leave. God, you put us all on edge yesterday. If I go to school, I can spend time with your daughter, and she will feel a little better."

"That's good. Yes, you go. But let me be clear about one thing: I will disburse the bills, whatever amount comes to, when I am released," Arpan insisted.

"If you utter another syllable, I will never come to you again," Srimoyee retorted.

"Have you lost your mind, Srimoyee? Your upcoming wedding costs have to be taken into account. Why will you spend a large amount of money on my treatment?"

"Don't always harp on my upcoming marriage and ridicule me. Besides, I have saved a tidy sum over the years. I have sufficient resources to run our mother-daughter family comfortably. I have more than enough savings to pay for your medical expenses at the nursing home. The discussion ends here, and I refuse to hear any more after this."

"Why would I taunt you, Srimoyee? Whatever I am saying is a fact. You're going to marry someone else soon. If he finds out you're doing this for me, will he like it?"

Srimoyee got up, walked to the exit, pushed the glass door open firmly, and left without looking back or exchanging another word. Every time she heard the word 'marriage', she felt overwhelmed. She could not control herself. On her way out of the nursing home, Srimoyee went to meet Dr Basu in his office. She knocked at the door and asked, "May I come in?"

"Oh yes, please come in, dear. Did you meet your friend? Listen, your friend has a medley of medical conditions. He needs to be under observation. This time, he suffered from a virulent strain of viral infection. However, he is responding well to medication and by tomorrow, I hope he will be a lot better, but he will need time to recover fully. He is a chain smoker and has problems with his lungs. I have scheduled a few pathological tests for him today, and once the reports come, I can be sure about my diagnosis. Will you be going to school now?"

"Yes, *Kakababu*, but please don't hesitate to call me if you need anything."

"Okay. Take care," Dr Basu assured as Srimoyee got up to leave.

Chapter 6

School got over at 1.30 pm. When Srimoyee spotted Ganga waiting outside the school gate, she handed Sagarseni over to her. "Please be very careful when you cross the road," she urged.

Sagarseni walked over to Srimoyee and said, "You are a very good, Miss. Ganga *Pishi* (auntie), you will cook my food like Miss did, okay?"

Srimoyee said, "Listen, your father is doing fine and will be back home with you very soon. You have to be a nice and responsible girl for the next couple of days and take care of everything with Ganga *Pishi*. If you feel upset, call me."

Srimoyee turned to Ganga and said, "Ganga, please take care of her. Call me if you need anything. Tomorrow is Saturday, so there is no school. The day after tomorrow is Sunday. Sagarseni, try to complete all your school homework yourself, but if you get stuck and can't figure out how to proceed, you can call me. Be careful," she briefed them and let them go.

After seeing off Sagarseni and Ganga, Srimoyee boarded a bus and headed to the nursing home. As expected, Dr Basu was not in his chamber at that time. It was 2 pm, and Srimoyee did not want to call up and disturb the elderly physician. An experienced and efficient matron, who had been part of the organisation for a long time, was in attendance in the afternoon. She was a little cranky and short-tempered, but was good at heart. Srimoyee knocked on the matron's cabin door and asked, "Sister, may I come in?"

"Come in," she responded in a matter-of-fact voice.

Srimoyee entered the cabin and got right to the crux. She asked politely, "Ma'am, I have come to enquire if the lab reports for the patient in cabin number 5 have arrived. If so, could you please share the details?"

"He is Dr Basu's patient! We can't tell you anything until he goes through the reports," the lady responded curtly.

"Okay, I understand the protocol involved. But, could you please assure me there's no reason to worry?" Srimoyee asked desperately.

"I am sorry, Madam. Please come in the evening and meet the doctor. He will tell you whatever you want to know about your patient. It is not possible to divulge anything now."

Dejected, Srimoyee walked out of the cabin and plopped herself down on a couch. She felt miserable as she thought of Arpan's future. He was doomed and crippled both physically and emotionally. How would he survive and continue to lead a normal life? Srimoyee felt miserable.

It was mid-April, the beginning of *Baishakh* and Srimoyee sat there alone. The afternoon sky was overcast, and dark grey clouds loomed low. It was the beginning of one of the Nor'westers or pre-monsoon thunderstorms. Strong winds swayed the trees outside, and torrential rain formed a mist. Srimoyee felt a gust of wind, and she took off her glasses. She was engrossed in deep thoughts. Her train of thought was broken, and she realised someone was calling her, saying, "*Didi*, your phone is ringing in your bag."

A young nursing staff member was passing by, and she had probably noticed Srimoyee sitting in a pensive mood for a long time, isolated from the hustle and bustle of the world. She called her to draw her attention to the fact that her cell phone had been ringing incessantly for quite some time.

Srimoyee felt a little awkward as she thanked the sister, saying, "Oh, that's right! I didn't notice. Thank you so much."

Srimoyee took out the mobile phone from her bag. Bijon had called her more than 15 times. Her mind was in turmoil and on the verge of revolting against the upcoming wedding. Srimoyee was, anyway, reluctant to marry Bijon right from the word go, and now, after her chance to meet Arpan, her scepticism got the better of her.

Srimoyee picked up the phone unwillingly. Bijon's voice thundered from the other end as he demanded an explanation from her. "Where on earth are you? Just how busy are you that you don't have the time to pick up my call during the entire day? I've been calling you so many times, but you have been dodging my calls. What do you think of yourself? We are all set to marry in a couple of days, and yet, you are behaving so callously. Tell me, where exactly are you now? I will go and meet you there."

"I'm at the nursing home with my friend. I'm sending the address on WhatsApp, come over." Srimoyee hung up the phone without giving him a chance to converse further.

As soon as she disconnected the call, Srimoyee knew her mother would be waiting to reprimand her and demand an answer for misbehaving with Bijon. In most middle-class

Indian homes, when a daughter reaches marriageable age, mothers desire to get their daughter married and well-settled in conjugal bliss. They seldom consider the compatibility factor in a marriage. Their concern for their daughter's welfare is based on only one factor: whether the groom is capable of providing a financially secure life for their daughter. For all other factors, they know they have prepared their daughter to adjust and find a workable solution to keep the marriage going. It is expected of a woman to sacrifice her freedom and desire for a stranger, and that is what marriage is all about. A successful marriage is one in which the woman can find a desirable middle ground and strike a balance. It all depends on her ability to compromise, adjust, and sacrifice. She should keep her mouth shut, obey her husband, and endure everything meted out to her quietly. This is how it has been going on for generations, since time immemorial.

Weighed down by the tremendous pressure and the stream of sacrifices she is compelled to make, the woman gradually falls into the dark dungeons of depression. More challenges are thrown at her when children are born. Her condition worsens as her attention is divided between raising her children on the one hand and taking care of her husband's needs on the other. In her innumerable attempts to ensure a good and balanced life for others, she destroys her own.

Srimoyee was reminded of her senior colleague Meera Di. One day, during an animated conversation in the staff room, she said she had two sisters-in-law who were spinsters and lived with her and her husband. Meera Di often bought their favourite savouries on her way back home from school, but they never appreciated her kind and loving gestures. In fact, they never pitched in or reciprocated her love. Meera Di not only cooked all meals single-handedly for her family every day, but also made morning and evening tea and served them individually in their rooms.

Meera Di's husband always ignored her grievances and turned a blind eye to his sisters' behaviour. In fact, he warned Meera Di not to utter a word against his sisters. Meera Di had been married for seven years and had no children. She would often be criticised for her inability to bear children. Hailing from a low-income family, Meera Di lost her father within a month of her marriage. Since then, she had been living like this. The school was a haven for her, where she rediscovered herself as an individual.

Srimoyee reminisced about Beethika Banerjee, also her senior colleague in school. She married after a three-year courtship. However, things took an ugly turn when she discovered her husband was an alcoholic. Her life turned into a nightmare, and she had to bear abuse from her husband. She had defied her parents to marry the man, so her parents had severed all ties with her after her marriage.

Srimoyee inferred that Miss Sucheta Sanyal, her Principal Ma'am, led the most purposeful life. She chose to remain single, a fiercely independent woman working towards a goal she had set for herself. Imparting education and shaping future generations into good and proud citizens of the country was her mission in life. A born leader, Miss Sanyal had been contributing to community welfare with her devoted efforts. She commanded respect and love, and people looked up to her for guidance and inspiration.

Srimoyee went up and stood in front of Arpan's cabin. He was fast asleep under the influence of sedatives and high doses of antibiotics. He looked so frail. She had learnt that he had been neglecting his health for a long time, eating erratically and had been in a state of physical and mental decline. His failing health made him prone to infections. Srimoyee stood there and realised she would have to distance herself from Arpan in the presence of Bijon, who was on his way to join her. Bijon was short-tempered, crass and impolite. He could be rude and harsh at the drop of a hat, and Srimoyee feared for Arpan, who was still in a delicate state. If Bijon uttered harsh words in front of Arpan, it would affect him adversely. Arpan was not in a state to be provoked in any way. To make matters worse, Dr Basu had sent word that he would not come at his scheduled time and would be late.

Srimoyee stood outside the nursing home, waiting for Bijon. After almost an hour, Bijon's luxury car stopped at the entrance. He came out casually, whistling and swinging his car keys in his hand. He stood in front of Srimoyee and said, "Sorry, dear. It seems you've been waiting for me for a long while. I got stuck in the traffic snarl. Why have you been standing here on the road for so long? You could have just waited for me inside the nursing home. Come on, let's see which friend of yours has been hospitalised. How is he doing?"

"He's fine. He's sleeping now. What's the point of disturbing a patient? Let's go and sit somewhere else."

"That's better. I don't like these places. It's not my thing, you know. It makes me feel despondent. Seeing so many patients struggling to overcome their illnesses terrifies me.

How easily the body takes over the mind and instils fear," Bijon said.

"That is only a natural thought to cross your mind because of your infinite alcohol consumption."

"Oh, these happen occasionally, dear. In fact, I will give up carousing totally after we get married. I swear I will keep my word. I have been fond of you since my childhood. Girls find me appealing and flock to me, but you smite me. What is it about you that attracts me so much? Perhaps you remember that after my school-leaving examination, I went to your village home with my parents. I met you and fell head over heels in love. I had confided in my mother about my feelings for you back then. That is the reason why my father readily agreed to take you and your mother in and offered you a flat on rent when you were in trouble and came to Kolkata seeking shelter. Anyway, today I plan to discuss certain relevant issues with you. Let's go to a restaurant, sit there and talk. Get in the car."

Srimoyee got in the car. Bijon stopped the vehicle in front of the Bedouin restaurant in Gariahat and said, "This is a time-honoured restaurant, and I used to visit it frequently with my friends during my college days at St. Xavier's College. That's why I decided to drop in here. Let me first place the orders. What would you like to have? Shall we order Chinese?"

"Okay," replied Srimoyee.

Bijon ordered two plates of mixed chowmein and chicken manchurian. He took out a pack of cigarettes from his pocket, picked one and lit it. He looked at Srimoyee and asked, "Tell me frankly: what do you want to say?"

"To start with, please stop smoking here. This is a crammed place, and although it is empty now, other customers might walk in at any time. It is a public place, and I have an aversion to cigarette smoke."

"Oh, you will get used to it eventually. Okay, I am throwing it. But I find your behaviour peculiar."

"Why? In what regard?"

"You know very well we are going to be wed soon, and it is high time we complete the shopping and take care of the paraphernalia, but every time I ask you to accompany me for shopping, you studiously avoid going out with me. I have discussed with my mother, you don't need to work after marriage. What I earn is more than enough for a lavish lifestyle. You don't ever have to join the professional rat race. Besides, I won't stay in Bengaluru alone after marriage. You have to live with me, attend to my needs, prepare my meals and cherish and support me. Forget the cooking, I will hire a cook, but we do need to be together, don't we?"

"Do you have anything else to say?" Srimoyee asked nonchalantly.

"Yes, of course. There's a lot more to say, but let me hear you first," Bijon replied.

"When we landed in Kolkata from the village, we went to meet your father, the only person my mother knew in this city. Realising the difficult situation we were in, your father eagerly extended a helping hand and arranged for our stay in one of his vacant flats. During those early days, when we were struggling to make ends meet in an alien city, your mother often dropped in to share with us fresh, home-cooked food she made for her family. I spent sleepless nights on an empty stomach studying because I wanted to excel in my exams. The job was the result of my hard work and determination. I am definitely indebted to your parents for their unstinting support, and I do have a sense of duty and responsibility towards them. But that doesn't mean I will quit my job. My job is my passport to a secure future with my mother. I need the money to meet our family expenses. Your father helped us financially from time to time when I was still a student. After I got the job, I returned the entire amount to him. I love my job and really enjoy spending time with little children. I am a teacher, but I don't work just to earn a handsome pay cheque every month. The job gives me satisfaction and helps me take care of myself. It is my outlet for self-love, and hence, I will never quit my job. And, are you asking me to take up your responsibility? Are you a kid? Who waited on you for all these years when you led a bachelor's life in Bengaluru? You've lived alone, frequently travelled all over the country and abroad. Why are you suddenly reminding me of my duties and voicing your concerns regarding my job? I have decided to take care of my mother with my money, not yours, because now you may be willing to pay for her expenses, but is there a guarantee that tomorrow the tables won't turn and you will think of her as a burden and blame me for her upkeep?"

"Yes, I can clearly fathom what exactly you want. But don't bring up your mother in our conversation now. Your friend, who is admitted to the nursing home, lives in Kolkata. Did you have any intimate relationship with him? If there was anything, it must have been a long time ago; you shouldn't keep it going now. We're going to get married soon, and he's also married. But if you want to get involved in an extramarital affair..." Bijon left the sentence midway and looked at Srimoyee mockingly.

"Excuse me," Srimoyee stood up, livid. "You have been talking utter rubbish for a long time, which is beyond my tolerance, yet I have been putting up with you, but don't you dare utter a word about my friend. And remember, we aren't married yet. I am not your wife, and you cannot dump your baggage, emotional or otherwise, on me. I am free, and have the power and choice to call off this marriage and leave your house if I want."

"Oh, come on. Don't be so dramatic. How dare you act snooty, standing right in front of me? Where was your friend when you left the village under duress? From your sharp reaction, I have a hunch that you are actually in a romantic relationship with your friend," Bijon lashed out.

Srimoyee bolted upright and said, "I'm leaving, I don't feel like sitting and talking to you anymore."

"Wait. I have already placed the orders, and the food will be served soon. Eat and then go," Bijon commanded.

"I am not obligated to follow your orders yet. And yes, one more thing, I will think twice before marrying a hypocrite!" Srimoyee picked up her green leather bag from the table and walked towards the door in a huff.

Chapter 7

Srimoyee was apprehensive of a major showdown after returning home. She expected two conflicting parties: her mother on one side and Bijon on the other, both baying for her blood. She imagined how Bijon's parents would join him with arsenals, all set to strike her mercilessly. She felt exhausted and wished to defer the confrontation for as long as she could. She decided to kill time outdoors, but she had nowhere to go. She looked at her watch. It was 5 o'clock. She had half an hour to spare. Srimoyee decided to take a short walk to Gariahat market to do some window shopping, and then visit the nursing home to meet Dr Basu and find out about Arpan's health based on the lab reports.

Srimoyee reached the nursing home right on time and met Dr Basu, who was emerging from Arpan's cabin after checking on his progress. "How is he, *Kakababu*? Are all the reports okay?" Srimoyee sounded concerned.

"Yes, he is improving, but he has a heart problem. We have detected a blockage in his artery that requires immediate surgery. After the operation, he will be fine. Don't worry. But the present state of his heart is definitely concerning. However, after the operation, he has to be careful and comply with medical advice. If he follows a regular, disciplined lifestyle, he will recover fast and lead a normal, healthy life," Dr Basu replied.

"Do whatever you think is best, Kakababu, but please put him back on his feet," Srimoyee wailed.

"Don't worry so much, dear; I am here to see to that. It is quite late now, go home."

Dr Basu's reassurances did little to calm the storm brewing within Srimoyee. She was reluctant to leave Arpan in this state and go back home, but she was also aware that, at day's end, she had to return to her nest! She left the nursing home with a troubled mind.

The next morning, while Srimoyee was preparing Arpan's soup, she felt uneasy as her left eye twitched continuously. She was concerned. She firmly believed that the twitching of the eye was an indication of some impending ill omen. Her belief had no scientific evidence, yet she had held on to her superstitions since childhood. As soon as she opened the door to go out, she encountered Bijon standing right in front of her with his parents in tow.

Bijon's mother charged, "What is this I get to hear? Did you have a one-to-one conversation with Bijon yesterday? He told me you said that you would continue working and wouldn't stay with him even after your marriage. Look, I suggest that you go there and find a job if you want. You have sufficient qualifications, and it won't be too difficult for you. But why are you opposing him when he wants to take you with him to Bengaluru? If your mother wants to stay with you, she can accompany you, and if she wants to stay here, we will take good care of her."

"Auntie, can I ask you a favour? I'll discuss this when I get home. I am going to the nursing home, where visiting hours will begin soon. My friend is very ill. I made soup for him that I will drop off, then come straight back."

Bijon's mother retorted sternly, "No, we have given you a great degree of freedom. We have gone to great lengths for you. We had told your mother about this matrimony long ago. We liked you very much, and so did my son. You agreed then. Now that everything has been finalised, I have a feeling that you're trying to avoid the wedding."

"Auntie, we are deeply obliged to you for all your support. We didn't have a roof over our heads when we landed in Kolkata. I was able to attain my qualifications and advance my career through your invaluable assistance. I agreed to tie the knot primarily out of a deep indebtedness.

"But I can't quit my job. With due respect, I want to say something right now. If I forbid your son from drinking, will he do it for my sake? It's an addiction he won't give up, and for me, teaching in the school is my profession. I don't know if I'll get a job in Bengaluru at all. Besides, I won't leave my sick mother behind and go anywhere. These days, long-distance marriages are on the rise, and relationships succeed despite the distance."

Bijon's mother declared, "Listen, dear, I am not concerned about who does what, nor do I want to know, but what my son wants is important to me. You have to quit your job if that's what he wants."

"To tell you the truth, I felt bound to go through with the wedding due to a sense of indebtedness. You harboured us when we hit a rough patch. But that certainly doesn't mean I will relinquish all my wishes and desires, sacrifice my interests and happiness on the altar of obligation from now on. Also, let me share some information with you. You don't know everything about me. I don't know if my mother told you or not, and I had vowed never to open up to my mother about this, but the situation is forcing me to do so today.

"Before you decide to get your son married, you need to know this: I was once an orphan. My mother got me from an orphanage and adopted me when I was barely five months old."

"What are you saying?" Lolita screamed from the adjoining bedroom. She had been unwell for a long time, but Srimoyee's words hit her with such force that she sat on her bed.

"Don't get excited, mother. I know everything. I've known since the day you told Arpan's mother the truth. But I never revealed anything to you because you gave me the roots to grow and the wings to fly, something that my actual mother never did. She dumped me and left. I do not know how or where I was born. Ever since I became aware, I have known you as my 'mother.' You guided my first steps. I have been nurtured under your wings, and you are my guiding light. But it is wrong to conceal the past and marry off your daughter."

Bijon's father fumed as he addressed Lolita: "*Boudi* (sister-in-law), how could you cheat us like this? If I had known, I would never have agreed to my son's marriage to your daughter. What will people say when they hear this?"

Bijon interrupted. "Do you need to tell people, Father?"

"Shut up, you scoundrel. We have a rank and status in society. Besides, is there a shortage of eligible girls for marriage in the country? It is best to terminate this alliance. She is doomed to misfortune and will bring bad luck to our family! I do not like her behaviour or the way she speaks. Ending an unhappy union is preferable to a lifetime of misery. People will sneer at her." Bijon's mother hurled the words at Srimoyee in a fit of rage.

Srimoyee smiled and said, "Auntie, times have changed. If people know the reason for calling off the wedding, society will definitely not hold me responsible because I am not responsible for my birth. It is not my fault. It is the shortcoming of the woman who brought me into this world and then deserted me. Why should I be ashamed of her flaw?"

Bijon's father said, "You will vacate this flat tomorrow. I can't rent out this flat any longer."

Srimoyee felt angry and betrayed as she said, "Strange are the twists and turns of life. You were all so sweet and amiable a little while ago, eager to finalise the wedding, but the moment you heard that I was an adopted child, the table toppled. You didn't think twice before delivering your verdict, ordering us to vacate the flat overnight when you know my mother is ill and I do not have any relatives or close friends here to help. But that's okay. I will fix up something, and we will vacate the flat tomorrow. Now you may please go and leave us alone."

Lolita felt helpless. In utter desperation, she pleaded to Bijon's father from her room, "Oh *Dada* (brother), my girl is talking nonsense, please forgive her. I confess, I was at fault for concealing the truth from you, but you have watched Srimoyee grow up from close quarters, and you know she is a wise, compassionate, graceful and righteous girl who slogged hard to complete her academics and take up a noble career like teaching. Give me a chance, and I will convince her to accompany Bijon to Bengaluru after they get married. She will quietly adjust and adapt to the changes."

"No, *Ma,* I refuse to listen to you anymore. I will no longer compromise on anything in my life. You lie down and rest. Take the medicines. I will be back early today, and I will also have to scout for an accommodation again!" With these words, Srimoyee went out.

Chapter 8

Srimoyee was slightly delayed because of the showdown at home in the morning. It was already nine o'clock, and she started walking fast, wondering if she would be able to meet Dr Basu in the chamber. The nursing home was already very crowded; the elevator was packed with no room to stand. Left with no other alternative, Srimoyee decided to use the staircase. Just as she reached in front of the chamber, she saw Dr Basu coming after completing his daily morning rounds.

Dr Basu noticed Srimoyee. He smiled and greeted her cheerfully.

Srimoyee asked, "How is your patient now?"

"He is much better. Let's see how soon we can schedule the surgery. I'll be out of the station for a fortnight, so I have been thinking if we can plan his procedure earlier so he can be released. This morning, his wife came to visit him. Although I don't know any of his relatives, the lady was very agitated and throwing her weight around when I entered his cabin on my regular round-up. I was furious. He is a nice gentleman, but she is definitely not."

"I don't know her, *Kakababu*."

"Mr Mukherjee's fever subsided last night and has not recurred. However, he continues to have those sudden stabbing pains in his chest. You can go and see him."

Srimoyee was in a profound turmoil. She thought that it would not be right to go to Arpan's cabin. She imagined Arpan and his wife burying their murky past, forming a close bond and deciding to make a fresh start. Maybe Arpan's wife broke down in tears seeing his critical condition, and he embraced her and pacified her. Srimoyee chose not to enter his room. Instead, she decided to check the cabin from a distance and leave.

As she advanced, she noticed a crowd outside the cabin. Several attendants and nurses were busy discussing something among themselves. Torn between fear and curiosity, Srimoyee advanced towards the crowd. The cabin's glass door was open. A high-pitched, feminine voice was heard clearly. A heated argument was in progress.

Seeing Srimoyee, a young medic approached her and said, "Madam, all this while I was under the impression that you were his wife. But he insists that she is his wife. Just look at how she is interacting with a patient. Once we went in to tell her to calm down, she insulted us."

"How did you assume I was his wife? Did I ever say that? I'm his friend."

The nurse stood, hung her head and faced Srimoyee. Srimoyee could hear a shrill female voice demanding, "Sign this paper right away, or I will never let you go free."

"I won't sign anything because it's not my flat. It's my father's property, and I will never hand over that property to you," Arpan's voice could be heard amid the din.

Srimoyee sensed that this was a specific instance of domestic violence against Arpan, and she could not ignore it without pursuing legal action against the perpetrator. She would not let anyone destroy Arpan's life, not as long as she was alive and around. She took out her mobile phone from her bag and stood outside the cabin, turning on the recorder. Meanwhile, inside the room, the Mukherjee couple was engrossed in a heated argument.

"Arpan, I am asking you for the last time, will you sign the paper or not?" his wife demanded.

"What will you do if I don't?" asked Arpan.

"If you don't, I will defame you. I will spread the word that you are a despicable man, a lowlife, who tortures and abuses me. You harass me relentlessly, and you are involved in an extramarital affair with the person who admitted you to this nursing home. You know very well how convenient it has become these days to morph photographs to humiliate or blackmail victims. It won't take me a moment to upload posters of you two on social media and ruin your reputation. You are well aware of how efficient I am in these technological matters. I've framed many people before, so if you don't want your girlfriend to get falsely accused, then you'd better write the Santiniketan property in my name and get it registered. I promise to grant you a divorce this time because you will have nothing left to live for. You will go bankrupt and end up down and out, and I will set you free forever. If you want our daughter's custody, I will give it. I have no problem with that. Now, sign all legal documents and register the house in my name; otherwise, I will see to it that your mother ends up on the streets. I won't let her live in peace in the old-age home.

And you? I will ruin you completely." Arpan's wife did not mince her words as she spoke.

"I can't take it anymore, my chest hurts. The person who admitted me here is getting married in two days. Don't you dare utter a word about her. Give me the paper. I'll sign it."

Srimoyee turned off the recorder and entered the cabin. She walked to Arpan's bed and snatched the pen from his hand. Then she ordered, "Stop. You won't sign on anything."

She turned to Arpan's wife and said, "Madam, do whatever you want to do, but I won't let him sign it. The house in question is his ancestral property and a valuable asset which cannot be passed on randomly to just anyone. You go ahead and do whatever you want, but let me share some small information with you. Before entering this room, I called the police station next to the nursing home, and the police will be here any moment now. I won't let you step out of this room until the police arrive."

Arpan put his hand on his chest and screamed, "Pamela, please leave me alone."

Srimoyee said, "This is a case of domestic violence against a man. I will see how Mrs Pamela Mukherjee talks her way out of this case."

"You can't do anything to me. Do you have any proof?" challenged Mrs Mukherjee.

"I don't speak without proof. I know nothing is admissible in court unless supported by evidence," Srimoyee said.

"What proof do you have?" Pamela demanded to know.

"Don't assume me to be so naive."

Arpan intervened and pleaded with Srimoyee, saying, "Srimoyee, please leave this place and go away right now.

Don't involve yourself in these filthy matters. You have a future. You can't deal with her. She will drag you through the mud. She is a filthy, rotten soul."

Just then, a commotion was heard outside the room, and someone asked, "May I come in?"

"Oh yes, please come in, Inspector. I had called you," Srimoyee said.

The inspector glanced at Pamela and exclaimed, "Hey, this is the daughter of the famous dancer Irani Chakraborty!"

"Is the daughter of a celebrity above the law? Above crime?" Srimoyee asked.

"No, no, I didn't mean it that way," the officer felt awkward.

"Listen, Inspector. She tortures her husband regularly. Not only him, but she torments all other family members. No one feels safe in her presence, and she abuses them all. I have concrete evidence to support my statement. She is behaving boorishly with her husband, who is critically ill. Can't she be arrested on these charges?" Srimoyee demanded to know.

By now, a crowd had gathered around the cabin. Hospital employees, nurses, and several members of the public had started gathering. Seeing the police, several doctors also hurried into the cabin.

Dr Basu pushed through the crowd and entered the cabin.

He told the inspector, "As soon as I started checking up on my patient, she started disturbing both of us in various ways. She may be Mr Mukherjee's wife, but that doesn't mean she can just come and cause trouble like this. She ought to remember that this is not her bedroom."

A nurse re-joined, "I had warned her several times, asking her not to speak with the patient in a raised voice or argue with him. He has chest pain, and if he loses his cool and flares up, it can affect his condition adversely. All guns will be pointed at the nursing home, and we shall be persecuted for negligence of duty. But they are simply refusing to listen. If you don't believe me, Inspector, you can check the CCTV footage, where you will find the recordings."

Pamela Mukherjee interrupted and said, "Mr Mukherjee is my husband, and I can speak to him however I please."

Arpan had remained a silent spectator for so long. Still, when he could not control himself any longer, he blurted: "Tell me something, officer, in our society, when women are abused by their in-laws or husbands, everyone, right from their family members to neighbours, and even strangers, rushes to help — to express sympathy to the victim. But can you tell me why this doesn't happen to men? Both men and women can be victims of marital conflict and domestic discord. Just as demented men often sexually victimise women travelling in crowded public transport, similarly, men too face identical harassment. But society refuses to acknowledge this bitter truth and looks the other way when men suffer. It is always the man who is seen to be at fault, the perpetrator of violence in a marriage, always giving credence to the woman's wailings.

"This is my wife, Pamela Mukherjee, daughter of a renowned dancer. To this day, I, my mother, and even my little daughter cannot live peacefully because of her conduct. If any of us ever protest, she threatens us with dire consequences. She is a manipulator who blackmails us, saying she will commit suicide and blame us all for her death to ensure our future is doomed behind bars. She uses arm-twisting tactics to get her way. Are there no legal steps to ensure the rights of men like us who are introverted, can't speak for ourselves, and can't oppose? Are we to remain silent victims all our lives, waiting for the end when we can be released from all worldly woes, and till then, live as walking dead entities?"

"Wow, so now you are articulating your emotions so well!" Pamela Mukherjee taunted Arpan. She then turned to the police officer and said curtly, "Listen, officer, this is a family matter, and we will handle it internally. Please don't interfere in our personal matters. We don't require external assistance. Please leave us alone."

"I'm sorry, Mrs Mukherjee, but this is not going to happen. Now it has been registered as a police case," the inspector said.

"I am surprised. Are you really well-bred and hail from a cultured background, or do you carry your smartness in your outfits like a clotheshorse?" The Matron came forward and lashed out at Pamela.

The inspector said, "Listen, Mrs Mukherjee, you have to understand that this is not your bedroom. Had this been your bedroom, the police would not have barged in or interfered. This is a hospital where everyone must comply with the hospital's rules. These rules apply to all patients and their visitors. They are all witnesses to your violations. Please come with us."

Srimoyee said, "Please take her away on charges of breaking hospital rules, and I will go to the police station and register other charges. I will ensure that she can never torture and destroy Arpan Babu's life in this way in future!"

Chapter 9

The sun gradually rose in the eastern sky, blazing with all its warmth. The attendant closed the two adjacent windows of the room and turned on the cabin lights.

Looking at Srimoyee, he said, "Actually, it's time to sponge him, and I need to take him to the bathroom."

"Okay. But will you give me just a few moments? I'll have a few words with him and leave."

Hearing Srimoyee's request, the young attendant left the room. As soon as the room was empty, Arpan said, "What was the need to involve yourself in this murky affair? You marry and settle down, Srimoyee. I promise I will never contact you again."

"Now stop talking about these things. We will discuss these matters later. You get well first."

"Why are you asking me to stop? How long will you take care of me? Very soon, you will disappear from my life again, which is nothing more than a living hell for me. I have endured enough in this life; now I want to be released from the fetters of life," Arpan said in a dejected voice.

"Okay, in that case, we can lose ourselves together. I am not marrying, and I have already announced this at home today."

"But why? Why have you cancelled your wedding?"

"You will not understand the reason."

Arpan gazed at Srimoyee for some time and then announced, "Hey, you have been caught again!"

Srimoyee avoided his gaze and said, "There is a lot of work to be done now. I have to find a rented apartment and move in with my mother by the end of the day. I also have to punish the culprit who made your life miserable. No one can harm my friend and get away with it... not even his wife. No one has the right to do that."

Suddenly, Srimoyee saw Arpan getting up from his bed. She panicked and asked, "Hey, what are you doing? Why are you getting up from your bed?"

"Wait a minute." Arpan scrolled his phone for a contact number and said, "Save this number. This is my friend's number. Contact him. I'll also keep him informed. If you get the flat, you can shift tomorrow. This flat is close to your school and won't take long to travel."

Srimoyee said, "Okay, I will take your leave now. Bye then."

"If I insist that you don't go, will you stay back?"

"How's that possible? So many tasks are waiting to be done. Besides, this is a nursing home."

Arpan kissed Srimoyee's hand softly and said, "After so many years, I am transported back to my teens as the sweet, fragrant breeze is once again revitalising me with boundless joy. Do you still love me so much, you crazy girl?"

Srimoyee smiled and got up to leave. Just as she stepped out of the cabin, she met Dr Basu standing right in front of her.

"I have something to talk to you about. Come to my chamber," said Dr Basu.

"But *Kakababu*, I have to go to the police station right now."

"I am asking you to come to my clinic to talk about that. Come."

Dr. Basu led Srimoyee to his chamber. After they both settled down, Dr Basu said, "The impending battle will be a tough one. The most important thing is that you are going to get married soon. If the media gets a whiff of the juicy gossip, they will ensure that it spreads like wildfire. I'm worried about how your future in-laws will take it."

"*Kakababu*, I was about to tell you, I have cancelled the marriage. I realised we have different mindsets. Our approaches conflict, and I would not be able to adjust to them. So, from this perspective, there is nothing to worry about. However, we have been evicted from the house, and I have been served a day's notice to relocate. I'm worried about finding a new home and settling down with my mother. I've also pondered what you're saying. If the media focuses attention on this issue and sensationalises the story, all eyes will be on me. Curious eyes will follow me everywhere, from my school to wherever I am. But what is unjust and unethical is unacceptable. I can't tolerate the vileness, and if it means losing my job, I will accept that."

"Why are you mulling over this issue so much, *Didibhai*? Your uncle is always with you. But you have committed a serious mistake by not telling me about the eviction notice that you have been served. Listen, my big house remains vacant all year. You know I'm a wanderer, and don't stay in Kolkata for long; I spend most of my days travelling here and there. So, bring your mother and shift to my house tonight. Don't bring anything with you except a few clothes. Why did you leave your mother there after all the discourtesy they displayed? Do you think your uncle is dead, or is it that you can't accept me as one of your own?"

Srimoyee burst into tears. She struggled to control her emotions before she could speak. "We are alive because of you, *Kakababu*."

"Don't weep like that in front of me. I want to see my niece strong. She's not a fragile girl. Don't worry about your job. If required, you leave that school and apply elsewhere. I am confident you will get a job at any other school. But don't compromise with your morals and values. Whatever I have earned in my lifetime is enough for you and *Boudi* (sister-in-law) to lead a comfortable life. However, I also know that you would not like to give up a profession you love. Frankly speaking, I don't have any problem with your choices, but if you have to compromise or face antagonism and disrespect at your workplace, I will never tolerate it."

Srimoyee wiped her eyes and said, "Thank you, *Kakababu*. May I leave now? First, I will go to the police station, and then I will go home to pick up my mother and head to your house."

Dr Basu interrupted and said, "Don't say 'your house.' Instead, say 'our home'."

Srimoyee hurried to the police station. The Officer-in-Charge requested her to take a seat.

"Please file a written complaint against the lawbreaker. Although I have already framed charges, Mrs Mukherjee's mother has appointed her own lawyer. I am making sure that an offender like her doesn't get away this time. None of them has arrived yet. You can file a complaint and wait for them."

"No, Sir, I'm afraid I can't stay. I am in a hurry, so I will file a written complaint and leave now."

Srimoyee completed her task at the police station and hurried home. When she reached home, she saw that Lolita was running a high temperature. It was not possible to shift her under such circumstances, so she called Dr Basu and informed him. She said, "*Kakababu,* I will move tomorrow morning only if mother's health improves a little. At present, she is so weak that she can't get up and sit without assistance."

Dr Basu offered to visit her, but Srimoyee declined, saying, "No, *Kakababu,* I will take care. If there is any problem, I will call you at night."

"Okay."

The next day was Sunday. Srimoyee called for a cab and, at the crack of dawn, left the house and headed for Dr Basu's abode with her mother.

Dr Basu was overjoyed to receive Lolita and Srimoyee. He hummed joyfully as he moved around. Dr Basu called Hari Kaka, the Man Friday who held fort in this male bastion and ordered, "Hari, cook a very special meal for us today. After all these years, my house is finally pulsating with life."

Chapter 10

It was a bright, sunny Monday morning, the first day of the week. Dr Basu's house was now Srimoyee's new address. She got up early, before Hari Kaka woke up and entered the kitchen. She prepared a healthy oats recipe for breakfast. Then she took a bath and got ready for school. She was, for once, very relaxed about her mother. She knew Lolita was in safe hands. Kakababu would be at home today, and there was no need to worry about her health anymore. Before leaving for school, she woke up Hari Kaka and informed him about the breakfast arrangement she had made for all of them.

The school bell rang after prayer, and classes commenced. Before going to her own class, Srimoyee went to the primary section to meet Sagarseni. Mrs Bhattacharya, Sagarseni's class teacher, had not yet entered the class. Srimoyee entered the class and looked for Sagarseni but could not find her. She asked one of the students, "Where is Sagarseni?"

"She hasn't come today, Miss," replied one of her classmates.

Srimoyee felt sorry for the little girl and wondered how Sagarseni was weathering the intense storm. Adversity seemed to be following her everywhere, with her mother abandoning her, her father hospitalised in a serious condition, and she had to live under the care of a maid in that spacious apartment. Suddenly, an idea crossed Srimoyee's mind: what if Arpan's mother could be brought in here right away? Sagarseni would at least have the love and care of her grandma. She was in a dilemma and could not decide if it would be okay for her to call Arpan's mother, at least for Sagarseni's sake. She knew Ganga would have her phone number. Besides, if she went to Arpan's flat, she could also find out why Sagarseni had not come to school.

Srimoyee took out her mobile phone from her bag and called Ganga, her heart anxious for the little girl. "Hello, Ganga? Why didn't Sagarseni come to school today?"

"Oh, *Didimoni* (Madam), I just couldn't wake her up from bed and get her ready for school. I tried my level best, but she just refused to open her eyes." Before Ganga could complete speaking, Srimoyee heard Sagarseni's baby voice. She had obviously grabbed the phone from Ganga and said, "No, Miss, Ganga *Pishi* herself was fast asleep and didn't wake me up."

"Are you all right?" Sagarseni's voice was so reassuring that Srimoyee felt a heavy weight lifting from her chest. Moments before, she was tormented by dark thoughts swirling in her mind. "Please give the phone back to Ganga, dear."

When Sagarseni handed the phone back, Srimoyee said, "Ganga, from tomorrow, keep your mobile phone beside you when you go to sleep. I'll call and wake you up. And please share with me her grandmother's phone number."

"I can't read or write, *Didi*, and I don't know how to send numbers on the phone either," Ganga replied.

"That's fine. Just stay with the little one. Cook something nice. Make sure she's bright and cheerful. I'll go to meet Sagarseni after school," informed Srimoyee.

Srimoyee disconnected the call and went back to class. She decided to get Arpan's mother's phone number by the end of the day and contact her, asking her to move into Arpan's flat to be with Sagarseni, who was living alone and completely dependent on the maid. On her way to Arpan's flat from school, she stopped to buy chocolates and chicken momos and then headed straight to meet Sagarseni. Her heart yearned to see the girl. As soon as she rang the doorbell, and Ganga opened the door, Sagarseni dashed out and hugged Srimoyee tightly.

"Miss, will you take me to see my father?"

"They don't allow children inside the nursing home, dear. Your father will come home in a few days. Do you want to go out somewhere instead? Tell me where you'd like to go—I'll take you."

"Will you take me to Nicco Park, Miss? Every Sunday, *Baba* used to take me to a park. We used to take the rides together. It was so much fun."

"All right then, you and I will go one day," Srimoyee said with a smile.

"No… it doesn't feel nice without *Baba*."

"Okay, as you say. Now, here, take these packets. They are all for you."

Sagarseni beamed as she took the packets and walked towards her room. One look at the kid was enough to realise that she was not happy or relaxed as she struggled to adjust to her new reality. Nonetheless, she was trying her best to put up a brave front.

"Please come in, *Didimoni.* I'll bring you something to drink," said Ganga.

"Give me your phone for a moment, please," Srimoyee asked.

Handing over her phone, Ganga turned up the fan in the drawing room and walked towards the kitchen. From Ganga's phone, Srimoyee took Arpan's mother's number and called her. At first, she hesitated, but after the initial dithering, Srimoyee explained the entire situation in detail. After hearing everything, Arpan's mother said firmly, "I'm taking tonight's train. I'll be home by tomorrow. I can't tolerate this injustice any longer."

Feeling much relieved, Srimoyee returned home. It had been years since she'd spoken with Arpan's mother. Earlier, when they lived in the village, Srimoyee often visited Arpan's house confidently, and his mother used to be so warm and kind to her. But ever since she learned that Srimoyee was an orphan adopted by Lolita and her husband, she became aloof, distancing herself and her family from Srimoyee and her mother. Now, after all these years, she was full of repentance and admitted to Srimoyee with deep regret, saying, "I messed up everything, and that's why God has punished me like this. But my son didn't commit any crime — so why should he suffer such a cruel fate?"

Kolkata traffic snarls were a routine occurrence, and Srimoyee often reached home late from school as she commuted by public transport. Dr Basu had told her countless times to use the family car, but she always refused. This often led to dissent between them, following which Dr Basu would sulk in silence for hours. Srimoyee, however, simply could not bring herself to travel in style. So, every time Dr Basu mooted the topic, she would deftly avoid it.

As soon as Srimoyee got home, Dr Basu exclaimed, "Your breakfast recipe this morning was excellent, *Didibhai*! After consuming Hari's boring, tasteless food for so many years, my taste buds had given up. Your fabulous dish has revived me, and now I caution you, I will bother you now and then to cook something special, *Didibhai*. I'm a foodie and love good food! By the way, I've decided to operate on your friend tomorrow. We'll keep him under observation for a day and discharge him the day after."

"You do what you think best, *Kakababu*. But I didn't inform the school today—I'll have to go in tomorrow."

"That's fine! I'll schedule the operation for later in the day. You can come after school. And don't worry about anything—I'm here, and I assure you, everything will be fine."

Chapter 11

After dinner, Srimoyee went to her room. Handing Lolita her medicines, she said softly, "*Ma*, do you know, I spoke to Arpan's mother today after so many years. I had to—when I saw that child's face, I just couldn't stay silent."

Lolita smiled gently. "You did the right thing, my child. In times of trouble, we should lend a hand to those who are struggling. During crises, we must let go of past grievances. But tell me something—don't you have any complaints against me?"

"Complaints? Why would I?"

"For not letting you know the truth about your birth..."

"You shielded me from all harm. You made a sacrifice to ensure my happiness. You kept me safe in your arms all my life. I know you couldn't have lived without me—that's why you made that choice. You are my mother, my pride. That's why I never went looking for my biological mother. To me, she's as good as dead. A woman who abandons her newborn has no place in my life. It's late now—go to sleep, *Ma*. Don't recall those memories. Arpan's operation has been scheduled for tomorrow. Will you come to the nursing home?"

"Yes, if you take me with you. I really want to see the boy."

"I'll bring his mother along on my way back from school—she'll need to sign some papers anyway. Be ready by then."

"Your *Kakababu* said you should take the car. He'll reach the nursing home early in the morning and send the car back for you."

After school, Srimoyee took Sagarseni along and went to Arpan's flat. The moment she rang the doorbell, Arpan's mother opened the door. "*Thamma* (Grandma)!" cried Sagarseni, darting forward to hug her. After a long time, the little girl had finally connected with her nearest and dearest.

She finally found a cherished companion. Arpan's mother still looked much the same—even as the creases of time had intensified, she remained strong and dignified. As soon as Srimoyee stepped forward and bowed down to touch her feet, she held Srimoyee's hands tightly and said, "Please don't delay any longer, let's go quickly. It'll take time to get there, and I can't sit still anymore."

"Just a moment, *Kakima* (auntie), let me book a cab," said Srimoyee.

"I can take the bus. My legs still have enough strength," Arpan's mother replied.

"But, how can I let you travel by bus, *Kakima*? I can afford a cab now," Srimoyee said gently.

"Don't embarrass me further, child. I've learned my lesson. At the fag end of my life, I've realised, humanity is the epitome of existence, beyond that nothing matters. Family pride, status, arrogance, and stubbornness are vices that destroy people. Let's board a bus. Just hold my hand when we get down, that's all the help I'll need."

Srimoyee glanced at Arpan's mother—Shubhra Devi—from the corner of her eye and quietly booked a cab. Then she called for Ganga, "Can you please get me a glass of cold water?"

By the time Ganga returned with the glass, a message pinged on Srimoyee's phone. Taking a few quick gulps of water, she said, "If we go by bus, it'll take too long. Come, the cab's here—it's waiting downstairs."

A cab pulled up and stopped in front of Dr Basu's house. Lolita was already waiting for Srimoyee to take her to the nursing home. "*Kakima,* come down," Srimoyee said, holding her hand gently, and helped her out. Seeing Lolita, Arpan's mother, Shubhra Mukherjee, could not hold back her tears. She held Lolita's hand and said, "God has punished me because I once hurt you. Once I drove you out of the village, and that's why I've been away from home for so long. But this time, I will make amends. Arpan is my only son. I will not let his and my little granddaughter's lives become a hell on account of one person."

Lolita replied, "Don't worry, *Didi* (sister), everything will be fine. Arpan's operation will be performed by my brother-in-law, who is like a younger brother to me — and he's a renowned doctor in this city."

Sanatan, the driver, drove the car out of the garage and said, "Everyone, get in."

Chapter 12

All major city roads were congested due to political rallies and heavy traffic, and they were delayed on their way to the nursing home. After arriving at the hospital, Shubhra Devi completed the formalities and signed the consent papers, and Arpan was wheeled into the operating theatre. Seeing his mother and Lolita standing next to each other at long last, Arpan was moved to tears.

Shubhra Devi placed her hand on her son's forehead and said, "Don't you worry, *Babu*. Srimoyee has told me everything. Now let's see, who dares insult me or you."

Lolita also stroked Arpan's head affectionately. Arpan looked at Srimoyee in a dazed state.

Almost an hour had passed since Arpan was taken into the operating theatre. Srimoyee sat outside in the waiting area, lost in thought. Her reverie was interrupted when her phone rang.

She took the call. A stranger said, "Madam, I am the OC calling. Please come to the police station, right now."

"But I am in the nursing home now, and Arpan's operation is in progress."

"What happened? Who's calling?" Shubhra Devi, who sat beside her, asked.

Srimoyee said, "*Kakima*, the police officer investigating the domestic violence case, had called. He asked me to go to the police station right away."

"You stay here. I'm going. My lawyer, Mr Pal, will accompany me. I've already discussed the case with him. He will take it up. Give me the phone," said Shubhra Devi.

Srimoyee silently handed the phone to Shubhra Devi. She introduced herself to the officer and said, "Hello, I'm Arpan's mother speaking. I'm coming to the station with my lawyer right away. Will that be all right?"

She then turned to Srimoyee and said, "Inform me when the operation is over. Go and take care of Arpan. I'm leaving him in your care. Rest assured, I'll take care of the other things. I will not rest until justice is served and the culprit is punished. God has taught me a tough lesson. For all these years, I was made to believe that my son didn't want me in his house any more. I was heartbroken but decided not to contest the issue and agreed to shift to an old-age home. But now that I have come to know the physical and mental torture she inflicted on my son, I am not going to sit silently and endure this crime. When women are the perpetrators of abuse and domestic violence, they deserve the same punishment as abusive men. One thing comforts me, though: I know that with the goodwill and love of well-wishers like you, my son will surely regain a healthy, happy life. I'm off to the police station to register my statement and do penance for my sins. Meanwhile, Srimoyee, you take care of my son."

Hearing Shubhra Devi's words, a beam of sunlight pierced the profound void of her life. She felt the unbridled joy of springtime when new leaves appear on barren trees and nimble-footed Santhal youths dance in ecstasy. Srimoyee's mother, Lolita, had never been over-ambitious, nor did she want much for the love of her life, her daughter. She wanted a normal, healthy and happy life for Srimoyee, and to see her settled in happy domesticity. She only wanted a peaceful, contented life for her daughter. She never harboured great ambitions, never dreamed that her daughter would marry into a very affluent or aristocratic family. Lolita thought of Arpan and resolved to wait for his recovery.

Srimoyee stood staring at the sky through the black glass window. She was in a pensive mood and thought about how, with the onset of dusk, the birds headed for their nests, fatigued from skimming the clouds far away. All creatures, big or small, have a roof over their heads where they go back at the end of the day, because God, like Dr Basu, exists on earth. She felt immensely grateful because she had a roof over her head, a safe shelter. But now she yearned for a special corner in her heart that she would reserve for the person she loved and wanted to be close to. She wanted a friend, a confidante with whom she could openly discuss anything and everything without a care in the world; when darkness engulfs the world and everything feels strange and mysterious, she longed to melt in the arms of her paramour, who would hold her tight in his arms, support her and assure her of approaching daybreak and the beginning of a new day. She wondered if her dreams would ever come true. Yet, the moment Shubhra Devi's words reached her ears, countless lamps seemed to light up the darkness. But Srimoyee was sceptical because, somewhere deep inside, she believed her fate always played truant, and the thought filled her with fear.

Lolita sat with folded hands, meditating and praying silently. Suddenly, she opened her eyes, looked at Srimoyee and asked, "Sri, is the operation still going on?"

"*Ma*, have a little patience — it's only been about an hour. It'll be over soon. Look, the door of the operating theatre just opened."

Srimoyee rushed towards the operating theatre. The matron was the first to emerge from the OT. She was a stern lady who adhered to etiquette and conducted herself with propriety. Both patients and visitors preferred to keep her at arm's length. Srimoyee was also in awe of her and steered clear of her. However, this time she was surprised to notice a gentle smile on her face. The reason she was all smiles was clear — she knew that Srimoyee was closely related to Dr. Basu.

Lolita asked, "How is the patient?"

The matron replied, "Even God acknowledges Dr Basu's presence in the OT. Arpan Mukherjee is fine now; there's nothing to worry about. The operation was successful. He'll be moved to his cabin shortly. But you mustn't try to talk to him today."

About fifteen minutes later, when Dr Basu came out of the operating theatre, Lolita asked, "Brother, hope everything's all right?"

Dr Basu removed his apron and handed it to an attendant, and then spoke to Lolita. He said, "*Boudi*, the operation went perfectly well, but we will still keep him under observation. Even after he's discharged and goes home, he has to be on complete rest. An efficient nurse must be assigned to him full-time. He will require a special diet, and medicines must be given regularly. And, *Boudi,* I'll be a bit late getting home tonight — I have to attend two chambers — but of course, I'll check on Mr Mukherjee once he regains consciousness before I leave."

After being shifted to the cabin, it took quite some time for Arpan to come out of the effects of anaesthesia. When he finally opened his eyes, the first thing he saw was Srimoyee standing quietly in a corner. Lolita pulled up a stool beside Arpan's bed and sat down. Placing her hand gently on his head, she said with deep affection, "It's been so long since I last saw you, *Babu*. You used to frequent our home in the village and insisted on having your favourite sesame sweets that I would make."

As she spoke, tears welled up in her eyes. She wiped them and continued, "Don't worry anymore. You're going to be fine. But once you go home, you must take complete rest. You have a daughter — you have to recover quickly for her sake! Your mother was here just now; she's stepped out for a bit. She'll be back soon. You just get well soon, son."

Chapter 13

Mrs Shubhra Mukherjee emerged from the nursing home and, accompanied by her lawyer, Arun Paul, went to the local police station. As soon as she entered the station, she came across Irani Chakrabarty, Pamela Mukherjee's mother.

Irani stepped forward and addressed Shubhra Devi and said, "I know my daughter has misconducted herself, but if the chargesheets filed against her are not lifted, there's no way I can get Pamela out of this mess. I have to keep up my public image as well. If the news circulates, it will send shockwaves through the city, and I'll be ruined. I won't be able to live. She is, after all, your only son's wife, so I would beg you to reconsider everything and withdraw the case...!"

Mrs Mukherjee retorted, "My only son's wife? The woman who conspires to separate a son from his mother and dumps her own offspring? She turns her home into hell with late-night parties, free-flowing alcohol, and welcomes casual acquaintances and friends to spite my son. She mentally tortures her husband, extorts money and property, and threatens to kill him at any time or commit suicide if she can't get her way. Such a person is quite capable of murdering someone without remorse. And you call your daughter the 'Lakshmi' of the house? Your daughter is beyond forgiveness.

I have come to substantiate the charges already imposed on her. I want to register a case against her for tormenting an elderly woman like me."

Irani Chakrabarty pleaded, "*Didi* (Sister), I beg you — must I lose my reputation and dignity at this age for my daughter? I would be drowned in shame and indignity, and wouldn't be able to face the world again. Please forgive my daughter. I have asked her to consent to her divorce. After the divorce, I'll send her somewhere far away from the city, and ensure that she can never contact you in future. But please, don't punish her like this."

The inspector said, "Enough with the crying. This is a police station. Sit down, Mrs Mukherjee. Do not show any mercy to the accused."

Shubhra Devi said, "Inspector, since the accused's mother is heartbroken and begging for mercy, I would like to speak to her daughter once."

"But madam, I would request you not to withdraw this case. This matter has already caused a significant disruption. The offender must be punished — otherwise injustices against men will increase in this society."

"Inspector, do you think real punishment for a criminal is served simply by locking the perpetrator behind bars? That may be the punishment devised by the legal system, but if her conscience is not reformed, she will come back and harm my family again. Though I came with my lawyer to file a charge, after hearing Irani Chakrabarty's pleas, I feel it might be worth speaking to her daughter once. If her daughter agrees to my proposal, my family will be free forever from a terrible criminal."

"Very well — do as you wish."

The inspector rang a bell to summon a constable. A young policeman came in and said, "Come with your lawyer and follow me."

Accompanied by Mr Pal, Shubhra Devi went in and stood in front of the lock-up. The constable opened the door, and Pamela Mukherjee emerged with her head bowed. She had been behind bars for three days and already looked pale and haggard. Shubhra Devi asked her bluntly, "Are you willing to divorce my son?"

Pamela looked down and said, "I promise, *Ma* — I will leave you, I will leave Arpan and go away. For the past three days, I have been reviewing my actions and have realised what an awful offender I have been. Ever since I got married, I have left no stone unturned to make your lives miserable. I disintegrated the family; I was arbitrary and tyrannical. You endured everything, and not once did you ask me to leave the house. I never bothered to look at my little daughter. How is my daughter, *Ma*?"

Shubhra Devi smiled and said, "This is the first time you've asked about the child. So, the law of the land has managed to conquer your arrogance, then."

Pamela fell at Shubhra Devi's feet and began to weep. "I promise, *Ma,* I will take my daughter and go. I will not ask for anything. If you have the divorce papers ready, give them to me, and I will sign. But I cannot live without my daughter."

"But you've been living without your daughter all these years! If you seek your daughter's custody in the court, it will not be granted because you don't have a job, and if we produce evidence of your neglect towards your child, you will get no help from the law."

"I won't go to court, *Ma* — I'm only pleading with you," Pamela implored.

"But you know Arpan — he's the one who single-handedly raised the child since infancy. Besides, I will not give up my granddaughter either. She's the only girl in our family line. So I can have you released from here only on one condition, the one your mother also agreed to — that you leave Arpan and my granddaughter forever."

"Sagarseni is a part of my being — how can I live without her? I had deceived myself about the nature or impact of my actions, but now I can see everything clearly and am full of remorse. Please don't take my daughter away from me; give me one more chance."

"There's no time to argue. I've stated my condition. Now it's up to you. If you agree, sign the lawyer's papers. When the divorce papers are ready, they'll be sent to you — then you can sign them as well."

Pamela said, "I have no other choice but to agree. My mother won't be able to show her face for my sake, so I must get out of this hell."

Pamela wept as she signed the lawyer's papers.

Chapter 14

The darkest hour is just before the dawn. After a long time, Srimoyee woke up as she felt the warmth of the sun shining through the window, revealing the hues, textures and patterns. Her alarm was ringing. It was 5.30 in the morning. The phone pinged. Arpan's 'Good morning' message greeted her.

Srimoyee typed, "Haven't I told you repeatedly not to wake up so early? You need to recover fast, and then you can join the office. As long as you're at home, get some sleep. Ganga is there to get Sagarseni ready."

Arpan messaged back, "Come home once after school today. I really want to see you."

Srimoyee smiled to herself.

Then she typed, "Won't be possible today. I will go on some other day."

Srimoyee had mentally fast-forwarded the relationship, though she did not express it aloud. Had Arpan's mother opposed the alliance, she would have had to let go of all her hopes. There was no point in rekindling her passion or crossing the line of friendship. Arpan was recovering now, so it was best to avoid him for the time being. Yet Srimoyee knew very well that if Arpan insisted on a video call even once, she wouldn't be able to refuse him. So, she switched off her phone, got out of bed, quickly got ready, and left for school.

Srimoyee made it a practice to meet Sagarseni regularly during lunch break and chat with her. She brought home-cooked lunch for Sagarseni. Sagarseni loved the food Srimoyee brought for her. It was not just the food — children seek love, affection, warmth, and care. Whenever Srimoyee looked at Sagarseni's innocent face, her heart ached. Though she had a mother, she didn't — not really. A life without a mother is painful, and that little girl understood it well.

Srimoyee knew Sagarseni had seen her mother leave her, but Srimoyee had never known her own biological mother. Despite that, she was immensely curious to know about her. Srimoyee had received Lolita *Ma*'s love. But what about Sagarseni? The impact of her mother's departure on her young mind was clearly visible in her sad eyes.

That afternoon, Srimoyee and Sagarseni sat under a Flame Tree (*Kishnachura*) during lunch break. Srimoyee asked Sagarseni, "How is your father?"

"He's better now, Miss."

"Aren't you happy now that your father has come home?"

"I'm very happy, but even though *Ma* wasn't always home before, she used to come sometimes. Now she doesn't come at all, and she doesn't call me. It hurts me a lot. When *Ma* comes, I'll promise her I won't bother her anymore. But I will make her promise that she shouldn't leave home again. Miss, has my mother forgotten me?"

Unable to answer Sagarseni's agonising question, Srimoyee held her tightly in her arms and said, "I love you very much, my child. Whenever you feel hurt, just call me and share your thoughts with me. If you can't figure out something while studying, show it to me. If you ever want to eat something, just let me know. I'll send it for you. I'm your friend, alright?"

"You're very nice, Miss. If only my mother loved me the way you do, I would have been really happy."

Srimoyee could see how much the girl missed her mother. But she had no inkling of the preconditions that Shubhra Devi had set for Pamela at the police station, which authorised the police to release Pamela from jail. Yet, in her mother's absence, Sagarseni's life was getting submerged in loneliness so deep and harmful that it could push a child's mind into the pits of depression at any moment. But Srimoyee's hands were tied. She wondered how Pamela Mukherjee could be so indifferent and cruel to this innocent little girl. The fear and ignominy of imprisonment drove Pamela to consent to the divorce, but as a mother, didn't she think of her daughter even for once?

Srimoyee reached home a bit late after school. On her way back home, she stopped at a shop near the school to buy chocolates, chips, and pastries for Sagarseni. That shop constantly teemed with customers at that hour, and it took quite a while for Srimoyee to complete the transactions.

As soon as Srimoyee returned home, Lolita confided, "I've devised a plan. It's time for Arpan's check-up. What if Arpan comes to our house for the check-up instead of going to the nursing home? Then we can have a little get-together."

Srimoyee replied, "Your idea isn't bad, but ask *Kakababu* first — and also Arpan's mother." Saying this, Srimoyee walked towards her room.

Lolita was bubbling with enthusiasm and could not wait any longer. No sooner had Srimoyee left the room than she immediately called Arpan's mother. "Hello, *Didi,* it's time for Arpan's check-up. If you all come to our house this Sunday for lunch, then we will be delighted. My brother is usually at home on Sundays. I will tell him everything. Then he can do the check-up as well. All of you, please come on Sunday afternoon."

Shubhra Devi said, "I was also contemplating organising a small gathering. Look, I made an error once, and I want to make things right. Both of us are getting old, and hence, no work should be kept pending for the unforeseeable future. Arpan's divorce from Pamela is accomplished. I want my son to marry your daughter as soon as possible. I treated you unfairly once. But time has taught me to understand people. I could have told you this earlier, but I was waiting for Arpan's recovery and the completion of Pamela's divorce procedure. Arpan is on his way to recovery. He has resumed his regular activities and will be joining the office soon. I am going to consult a priest and finalise the wedding date. Prior to that, I intend to visit your house this Sunday to bless the couple. My granddaughter is crestfallen and keeps asking for her mother, so I want Arpan and Srimoyee to get married as soon as possible, provided that both Dr Basu and you have no objections to the alliance! I know for a fact that even to this day, both Srimoyee and my son love each other intensely. I am confident that Srimoyee will become a wonderful mother to Sagarseni."

After hanging up the phone, Lolita was brimming with happiness. She felt on top of the world. She now needed to speak to her brother, Dr Basu and break the news.

Dr Basu was sitting in his room, engrossed in reading a medical journal, when Lolita knocked on the door and asked, "Brother, may I come in?"

"*Boudi*, how many times have I told you — when you enter my room, you don't need to seek my permission."

Lolita avoided replying to Dr Basu's charge, saying, "Alright, I'm sorry, but you see, I'm getting old, so I can't remember everything. Anyway, I have something important to discuss with you."

Dr Basu put the journal on the table and said, "Tell me."

Lolita recounted everything to Dr Basu — their past and present.

Dr Basu sat silent, listening to Lolita intently. He then said, "I always felt that the chemistry between these two was more than just friendship, but I never said anything. Now that it's my *Didibhai's* wedding, my responsibilities have increased tremendously. There will be so much to arrange! They will also come for the blessing ceremony. Should I invite everyone from the nursing home on the day Arpan's mother will come to bless the couple, *Boudi*?"

Lolita replied, "There's no need for a lavish ceremony during the blessing ritual. Besides, Arpan is still convalescing. Let's make the blessing ceremony a small and intimate occasion. Later, we can make arrangements for a lavish wedding."

"Alright. Sunday is my day off anyway, but it's good you told me in advance. I'll cancel all other appointments."

Srimoyee was in her room, busy checking exam papers, when Lolita entered the room. She looked up from the answer sheets and asked, "Do you want to say something, *Ma*?"

"Are you busy?" Lolita asked.

"Yes, I am, but since you're here, please tell me."

"I called Arpan's mother. I have great news. All these days, I have prayed to the Almighty, and today, it feels like my prayers have finally been answered. Arpan's mother is eager to see you two get married. She said if they come to our house this Sunday, Arpan's check-up can be done, and she will also bless you for the marriage."

Srimoyee placed a paperweight on the answer sheets before her and stood up. "What are you saying, *Ma*? She has agreed?"

Srimoyee had sensed this possibility earlier when Arpan's mother spoke to her at the nursing home, but she was still doubtful, and that's why she had steered clear of Arpan all this time.

The moment she received this long-awaited news, she felt overwhelmed. She felt like a tiny rag doll that was being carried by massive waves in the middle of the ocean.

Since childhood, she had envisioned only one person in her dreams — Arpan. Arpan would be her companion for life, with whom she could share all her joys and sorrows. For a moment, Srimoyee drifted into a dream world where she imagined herself in a bride's attire, wearing *shankha–sindoor*, standing on the balcony and waiting for Arpan, who was returning home after a long day's work, smiling and waving at her as he opened the car door, his face lit by inner happiness and contentment, while a bashful smile played on

Srimoyee's lips. Lolita's coughing snapped her out of her reverie.

Lolita said, "But, *Ma*, you'll have to handle the entire responsibility of Sagarseni."

Hearing Sagarseni's name, Srimoyee trembled from inside. She hugged Lolita and asked nervously, "*Ma*, will I really be able to take care of her? Will she accept me as her mother?"

"You take responsibility for so many children at school, and you're scared to take responsibility for just one more? And she loves you!"

"She loves me, yes... but will she give me her mother's place? I'm very scared — very unsure."

"Don't worry. We will all help her understand. Arpan will explain too. She will accept you eventually."

It was Sunday. Hari Kaka had been up since morning, dusting, cleaning and decorating every corner of the house elegantly with all kinds of flowers. Srimoyee laughed and asked, "Hari Kaka, the house already looks like a wedding hall today."

"It is a wedding home! That's why I decorated it lavishly. Don't you like it?"

"It's wonderful, Hari Kaka. I'll go and get ready now."

As soon as Srimoyee entered her room, she saw Lolita waiting for her with a gorgeous saree and several jewellery boxes in her hands.

"Do you want to say something, *Ma*?"

"Take this saree, and all this jewellery—your *Kakababu* sent them. Wear these today. And, one more thing: remember that the blessing ceremony doesn't mean the wedding is complete. So, you must try to maintain restraint. Just because the blessing ceremony is accomplished, it doesn't mean you meet Arpan too frequently. Too much proximity will reduce the charm."

"*Ma*, after all these years, our mutual attraction remains intact. So, if we meet now and then a couple of times, the appeal won't disappear either. But since you've said so, I will obey you."

Lolita said, "Things that are attained easily lose their charm, Sri."

The doorbell rang, and Hari Kaka opened the door. Srimoyee peeped from her first-floor balcony and saw Arpan dressed in a maroon kurta—just like a prince from her dreams. She whispered to herself, *"Touch wood, may my eyes never cast a bad omen on him."*

Sagarseni was holding her father's hand. Behind them was Shubhra Devi.

Lolita rushed out of the kitchen to welcome them, saying, "Come, come, *Didi*." She welcomed them warmly and seated everyone in the drawing room. Hari Kaka stood ready with glasses of *sherbet* as welcome drinks.

Dr Basu emerged from his room. He sat next to Arpan on the leather sofa and asked, "How are you now, handsome young man? Let me do your check-up first."

Sagarseni said, "*Thamma* said we were coming to Miss's house, but I can't see Miss here!"

Hearing Sagarseni's voice from upstairs, Srimoyee came down and stood beside her.

Sagarseni said, "Miss, you are looking very pretty."

Srimoyee lovingly replied, "Well, that may be true, but I am still not looking as beautiful as you."

Everyone burst into laughter.

Sagarseni said, "Your house is very big—so many lights, so beautiful! Where is your room?"

"Upstairs. I've brought many gifts. Come, I'll show you."

Looking toward Shubhra Devi, Srimoyee said, "*Kakima*, please come to my room."

"I'll come later. Let me pitch in the kitchen and help Lolita a little first. We are already very late. If we had arrived earlier, I could have helped her with the cooking!"

Lolita quickly replied, "Everything is ready. We have been waiting for all of you to arrive and then sit down and dine. I've cooked very light food for Arpan, and no spicy items for Sagarseni."

After finishing the check-up, Dr Basu said, "Arpan is doing perfectly well, no issues at all. But please avoid rich food. Try to maintain a disciplined lifestyle."

Shubhra Devi said, "I am certain that the person I'm entrusting Arpan to will be able to take complete care of him."

Srimoyee lowered her head shyly.

Shubhra Devi then urged, "Let us begin the blessing ceremony first."

Lolita added, "*Didi*, my brother and I have also decided to bless Arpan today. We don't want to delay and keep things pending either."

"Good, that's very good. Today is an auspicious day as well."

Srimoyee and Arpan were seated next to each other in two chairs. A lamp was lit beside them. Various items required for the ritual, including rice grains, sacred grass, incense sticks, flowers, and a plate heaped with sweets, were placed in front.

Arpan's mother, Shubhra Devi, blessed Srimoyee with an exquisitely crafted heavy gold jewellery set, studded with precious gems and an expensive saree.

Lolita blessed Arpan with a gold ring. Dr Basu blessed Arpan and gifted him a gold chain and a premium wristwatch. Once the blessing ceremony was over, Sagarseni said, "Come, Miss. Now show me your room."

Srimoyee looked at Arpan and asked him to accompany them.

Srimoyee's room was in the south-east corner, on the first floor. Pushing open the black glass door, Srimoyee entered her room and ushered in Arpan and Sagarseni. Her bed was heaped with gifts. Looking at Sagarseni, Srimoyee said, "All these are your gifts. Open them and see if you like them."

Sagarseni replied, "If you like them, then I will surely like them too."

Sagarseni was as polite as Arpan himself. Srimoyee said, "Sagarseni, you can call me '*Mamoni*'."

"Why, Miss? You are my Miss. One of my friends calls her mother '*Mamoni*', but you are not my mother."

As soon as she said that, Srimoyee felt a sharp little prick in her heart. It was true indeed, but she was not prepared for such a reply.

Arpan immediately hugged Sagarseni and said, "Imagine if from now on, Miss becomes your *Mamoni*, how would that feel?"

Without answering Arpan, Sagarseni said, "I'll look at the gifts first, *Baba*."

Arpan placed his hand on Srimoyee's shoulder and said, "Give her a little time. Everything will be fine."

"Let's sit outside on the balcony." They pulled out two chairs and sat next to each other.

"You are looking stunning today. Occasionally, when you dress up a little, you look gorgeous!" Arpan commented.

Srimoyee laughed, "Why should I dress up again just for you?"

"That's true, but sometimes I also like to see you looking nice."

"I'm thinking about one thing," Srimoyee said. "Sagarseni is unhappy and misses Pamela. She might find it difficult to see me in her mother's place. That could create pressure in her mind."

"You're still thinking about this? Everything will be fine."

"Arpan, you don't understand. There's a vast difference between one's own mother and a foster mother. I've never seen my biological mother, so I have no feelings for her, but Sagarseni has known her mother. Will she be able to accept me?"

"Stop thinking about all this nonsense." Arpan took Srimoyee's hand and kissed it. He said, "I feel so romantic today. I really want to pamper you."

Srimoyee felt a mix of shyness and joy, almost wanting to lose herself in the moment. Arpan got up from the chair, took her hand, pulled her close, and embraced her, kissing her deeply on the lips. Then he took a diamond ring from his pocket, slipped it onto her ring finger, and said, "You, only you, are my forever."

The shrill sound of the calling bell jolted Srimoyee out of her trance. Lolita had called her several times, but when she did not answer, Lolita decided to ring the doorbell. Srimoyee released herself from Arpan's embrace and said, "Come on, they're waiting for us. They are calling us for lunch."

Arpan said, "I don't want to let go…"

Srimoyee disentangled herself from Arpan's tight embrace and went back to her room, followed by Arpan. Sagarseni was playing with a Barbie doll.

"How do you like the gifts? Tell me, Sagarseni."

"They're lovely, Miss."

"Take them home when you leave. Now come, *Dida* is calling. We have to go downstairs and have lunch together, right?"

Srimoyee picked up Sagarseni in her arms and went downstairs.

Shubhra Devi announced, "We have finalised the wedding date for the 28th of November. Arpan and Srimoyee, both of you, do the needful to apply for leave from your workplaces as per your convenience."

It was the first day of the week, and Arpan went to his office. Srimoyee was at school and had a strong urge to call him repeatedly. But she knew Principal Ma'am was a strict disciplinarian and did not allow teachers to carry mobile phones during classes.

During lunch break, all the teachers surrounded Srimoyee in the staff room. After joining the school, Srimoyee bonded well with her colleague, Raka Chatterjee, and they became very close.

Raka said, "Why are you so perturbed, dear? The wedding is only a few days away. After that, you will have him to yourself permanently, 24*7. For now, at least pamper yourself and visit the beauty salon occasionally. You need to give yourself a little time, too."

A scared Srimoyee urged her to keep quiet, "Shhh, someone might hear."

"Everyone already knows about you."

"Of course, it's all your doing. You can never keep a secret anyway."

"And what's the point of hiding it, huh? You'll have to invite everyone, right? Even our Principal Ma'am, right?"

"Of course I will. I am really fond of Sanyal Madam."

Ajanta Di was a senior teacher. She called the other teachers and suggested, "Why don't we treat Srimoyee to a special feast before she ties the knot? My house is empty, so if all of you agree, we can decide on a Sunday and organise the event. We'll cook ourselves and feed her."

Raka was very excited. She said, "That's wonderful! There's not much time left anyway—just one month. After Diwali, our friend's life will truly light up. Tomorrow and the day after, we will be busy with excursions for the ninth- and tenth-graders. After that, the Puja holidays will begin. And when the Puja holidays are over, it will be time for her wedding. Srimoyee, will you accompany us for tomorrow's excursion?"

"Didn't you notice my name on the list?" Srimoyee laughed.

Raka had a grave expression when she said, "I thought your groom might not let you go with us?"

The staff room was in a celebratory mood, filled with joy and laughter.

Chapter 15

After a two-day school trip, Srimoyee returned from Jalpaiguri. As soon as she rang the doorbell, Hari Kaka opened the door. Lolita was relaxing on the sofa, watching her favourite television soap. Seeing Srimoyee, she said, "Why are you so late?"

"The train was late, *Ma*."

"Have you been able to contact Arpan? He was looking for you. He tried calling you many times, and when he couldn't reach you, he came to our house."

"When?"

"Last night."

"There was no network there." She put down the heavy bag she was carrying and went into the washroom to splash water on her face. Srimoyee asked, "Did Arpan come for anything important?"

"Sagarseni is apparently very unwell."

"What's wrong with the girl again?"

"I've been waiting for you. I planned to go to their house with you once you returned."

"Then get ready. I'll go and change because this outfit is soaked in sweat."

Dr Basu had taken the family car to the nursing home. Srimoyee booked a cab and reached Arpan's flat with her mother. Shubhra Devi was astonished to see Lolita and Srimoyee standing in the doorway. She hesitated initially and then said, "Please come in. Arpan hasn't returned from the office yet."

Srimoyee said, "We haven't come for Arpan, *Kakima*. Actually, Arpan had called me several times over the last two days, but I was away on a school excursion. There was no network there. I just returned this evening. As soon as I reached home, *Ma* told me Sagarseni was very sick. Arpan had visited our house last evening to inform us about Sagarseni's illness. So, we stopped by to see her. If you don't mind, may we go inside? Can we see the girl once? Is she sleeping?"

"She is in that room with Pamela, who is feeding the child now."

Lolita's countenance fell. In a faint voice, she asked, "Pamela?"

Shubhra Devi said, "Her fever had been very high for the past three days. In her delirium, she kept screaming for her mother. The doctor said her mother should be brought to her as soon as possible; otherwise, it could lead to traumatic brain injury. So, I had no choice but to summon Pamela. Now both mother and daughter stay in the same room, eat together, and sleep together. Sagarseni is responding to the medical treatment and is gradually improving. But, ever since Pamela came, Arpan returns home late at night, concludes his meal and shuts himself in his own room for the night. He wakes up early and leaves before sunrise. I truly don't know what to do in such a situation. To be honest, Arpan loves the girl very much, too. We have no control over God's will."

Lolita's brow furrowed with anxiety. Srimoyee comprehended very well that this situation was unacceptable to Lolita. She placed her hand over Lolita's ice-cold hands. Lolita was terribly worried about Srimoyee and the consequences of the arrangement she would have to face.

Shubhra Devi said, "Every night, Arpan spent considerable time talking with Sagarseni, telling the little girl stories that included Srimoyee, so that she would accept Srimoyee, but the kid absolutely refused to accept it. Once she gets better, both Arpan and I will explain everything to her again. Don't worry, Lolita. When we've given our word, this marriage will happen."

Srimoyee interrupted her and said, "*Kakima,* let's not talk about all this now. I just want to see Sagarseni once. The child is so ill. Why are we bringing up these matters now?"

Lolita said, "Won't you ever think about yourself?"

"*Ma,* you too? Then listen, regarding Arpan, I will do what I feel is right, and believe it will be good. May I go inside now, *Kakima*?"

Srimoyee knew that Shubhra Devi had kept her waiting in the drawing room for so long precisely to hear this from her. Over time, Srimoyee had learned to read the minds of people around her.

As soon as she pushed the door slightly open, she saw Pamela feeding and gently stroking Sagarseni's head while keeping her engrossed by telling her fantastic fairy tales. Sagarseni listened intently to her mother as she fed her. Once the child had finished eating, Srimoyee entered the room.

Sagarseni shouted, "Miss, you've come? Look, my mother! I told you my mother doesn't love me, but look—she came, she's telling me stories, she's feeding me. Mother said she'll never leave me again. You once told me everything would be fine. Today God fixed everything."

Gently caressing her, Srimoyee said, "Now you're happy, right? Both your mother and father are with you. Get well soon."

Overjoyed, Sagarseni climbed onto the bed and began playing with her doll.

Pamela said, "I've heard your marriage to Arpan has been arranged. I don't want to come between you two. I only want my daughter."

Srimoyee asked, "What will you do if Arpan states he wants Sagarseni? You two don't want to stay together, yet Sagarseni wants both her parents equally. She doesn't want any third party to come in between. When you brought a child into this world, it was because both of you wanted her. So, is it right to shy away from your responsibilities as parents just because you and your husband don't get along? Why can't you both set aside your pride, your grievances, your ego, and live together—for the sake of this little child? These children are the guiding star of the future."

"I feel like conversing with you and sharing with you many things today, but this isn't the right time. If I call you someday or ask to meet you somewhere outside, will you come?"

"That's for later—we'll see." Without saying anything more, Srimoyee left the room.

Going over to Lolita, she said, "*Ma*, you can go and see her once. You were restless to see her."

Lolita said, "Yes, since I've come all the way, of course I'll go and see her."

Removing her glasses and wiping her eyes, Shubhra Devi said, "Yes, please go."

Once they returned home, Srimoyee locked herself in her room. She was devastated. How many more battles was she destined to fight in one life, she wondered. She switched off her phone and lay on the bed, weeping inconsolably, and fell asleep. She woke up when she heard Arpan calling her.

"Open the door, Sri. I have a lot to tell you."

Srimoyee did not respond. Hearing Arpan's voice, Lolita came out of her room and said, "Let her be alone today. Getting beaten down by circumstances has worn the girl."

"Is she the only one hurt, *Kakima*? What about me?"

"Look, Arpan, you are a father. Before anything else, your responsibility is to raise your daughter properly. Suppose you marry Sri, but the child refuses to accept her as a mother under any circumstances. What will that lead to? She will grow up and always blame you and distance herself from you — you won't find peace in that, and neither will Sri. Raising a child is a daunting challenge.

"Consider your daughter once. All these days, she has suffered and wailed inside for her mother. Right now, you may feel that everything will work out, but in reality, it doesn't happen that way. If you force her, it will put pressure on her mind and will be detrimental to her normal growth. My experience is far greater than yours. For a moment, even I thought she might accept Sri as her mother, but now I realise it is not possible. And from what I know of my daughter, she will never do anything that harms you. So go now. When Sri gathers herself, she will definitely contact you."

"*Kakima*, I can't live without her. I have a life of my own, too — a right to live it with the person I love. I want to tell you something. Yesterday, Pamela told me she wants to leave with our daughter."

"Will you be able to live happily without Sagarseni? Ask yourself again and again. I know you truly love Sri, but sometimes in the conflict between love and duty, duty must be chosen first."

"I did fulfil my duty, *Kakima*. Pamela tormented us so much, yet I endured it."

"Didn't Pamela apologise to you, Arpan?"

"Last night, Pamela came into my room. She apologised. She said she's too embarrassed, and can't show her face to me, but even then…"

Wiping her eyes, Lolita said, "Life is a strange school of experiences. It is like a game of cards. We don't choose our circumstances, but we do choose how we handle them. We are merely puppets in the hands of destiny. Take the present situation, for example—the child fell ill and wanted her mother; this was perhaps an indication of a hidden blessing coming your way, or maybe a result of some past karma."

"I have never knowingly harmed anyone in my life, *Kakima*, then why should I deserve such karma? And, even if a broken relationship is mended, a broken heart never truly heals."

"Perhaps it doesn't, but in some situations in life, one must sacrifice one's self-interest. I'm not feeling well. Go home now, Arpan. Sri will definitely contact you. She is a very strong-willed girl."

Arpan left with a heap of disappointment. Lolita called, "Sri, open the door. Arpan has left."

Unlocking the door, Srimoyee came out and collapsed into her mother's arms, weeping.

"*Ma,* why does fate deceive me like this every time?"

Lolita said, "You are tough and courageous, and God tests your resilience, and see how you remain steady in the face of the fiercest storms! I've been mulling over something all this time. Perhaps you were born for a greater purpose. Destiny will possibly drive you somewhere far greater than the mundane domestic married life. God doesn't wish to bind everyone within four walls. Look at your *Kakababu*—he works for the people, for the country. In the same way, maybe God has sent you to this world with some specific purpose. You will be the beacon of hope for millions of unfortunate destitute, who are groping in the dark, seeking love and shelter."

"It's quite late now, and you must be starving. Come, I will feed you with my own hands tonight."

Chapter 16

Srimoyee gazed at the vast blue sky through her window. Soft white clouds wafted across the clear, deep blue sky. The autumn air carried the whiff of the upcoming Durga Puja. There was a flurry of activity in every neighbourhood; Puja pandals were nearing completion. Srimoyee and Arpan had earlier planned to go shopping for the upcoming wedding on this day – plans that seemed like a memory from her past life.

Srimoyee smiled to herself, thinking how unfortunate she was, because misfortune seemed to follow her everywhere. She picked up the books and papers on the table and shuffled them around for a while, but could not concentrate. Turning on her phone's network, she found nearly twenty-five WhatsApp messages from Arpan. Suddenly, a call came from an unknown number. After hesitating for a moment, she finally answered it.

From the other end came Pamela's voice. "Hello, this is Pamela speaking. Please give me just two minutes to talk."

"We spoke about everything only yesterday—why again?"

"Yesterday, I couldn't say everything. Please give me just two minutes. At least once in my life, I want to confess everything to someone. A month after my marriage, I found out that Arpan didn't love me—his heart belonged to someone else. His family forced him to marry me. From then on, I began to feel that what he and his family had done—getting me married without telling me the truth—was a grave injustice. In an arranged marriage, two strangers usually need time to get to know each other. But when I tried to use that time to get closer to him, I realised I had been deceived. After that, I changed myself completely. I felt deceived and bitter. I was determined to punish all those who had ruined my life. I berated my mother-in-law, fed her lies about Arpan, and drove her out of the house. After she left, I began to torment Arpan mentally, but I didn't realise that in all this, my little daughter's life was being destroyed. When I spent two nights in jail, my daughter's frail face haunted me. I asked my mother-in-law to give me my child so that Arpan could begin life afresh, with no strings attached. But I also knew that Arpan could never live without his daughter. So, I accepted all conditions imposed on me and went into exile."

"What is the reason for telling me all this? I already told you yesterday, when you bring a child into this world, both parents must take equal responsibility for the child's welfare. Love has the power to heal even the deepest hurt, and Arpan is a soft-hearted man. If you had loved your daughter, cared for Arpan and his mother, your family would have prospered and flourished too. Such incidents are not unique in this world, but you chose the wrong path. With patience and love, you could have earned Arpan's respect, affection, and love. What you couldn't do before, you can still try to fix now. A relationship does not end just because of a signature on a piece of paper. Walk the honest path, protect this family with love. That is where you will find peace."

"I have realised my blunder only now. I was filled with an intense rage and jealousy towards you. But today, after talking to you, I understand why someone like you remained in Arpan's heart – it is natural. As a human being, you are amazing and much more generous and selfless than I am. I do not have a heart like yours. You deserve Arpan. I want your marriage to take place. If you can explain things to my daughter to accept you for Arpan's sake, then I will not show my face again, even if Sagarseni asks for me."

"You may not know this, but I am no longer going through with this marriage. The rest is for you and Arpan to decide – whatever you feel is right. You never need to call me again. I wish you both well. But I must meet Arpan once." Letting out a long sigh, Srimoyee ended the call.

Arpan's office was close to Princep Ghat, on the bank of the Ganga River. On Saturdays and Sundays, the place gets crowded, but on weekdays, it remains peaceful. Choosing a secluded spot, Arpan and Srimoyee sat down next to each other.

Arpan took a cigarette out of his pocket, lit it, and asked, "So what have you decided? You're going to leave me. Right?"

"You're looking very weird, Arpan. Your hair is messy, you haven't shaved properly, and you've come to the office wearing such a faded shirt!" Srimoyee observed and commented.

"Leave all that. Why did you call me?"

Srimoyee took out a jewellery box and handed it to Arpan.

"Keep this box. *Kakima* gave it. The gold necklace that *Kakima* blessed me with is inside, and also your ring."

"You had to return these? That necklace is my mother's blessing, and the ring is my love. Was it becoming too much of a burden to keep them?" Arpan sounded hurt.

"You won't understand, Arpan. You can't have an answer for everything."

Srimoyee turned her face away. A torrent of tears streamed from her eyes.

Arpan held Srimoyee's hand and asked, "Can't we think it over one more time?"

"I've fortified my heart. Okay, you tell me one thing—suppose we were to build a life together, there's no guarantee that it would be filled with only love. Perhaps, for some unspecified reason, our love could fade. And just because we love each other, is there a rule that we must always stay together? I know, I can never really forget you in my life. I know you can't either. Maybe we'll remain like this, living in each other's hearts. Everyone in life has their own place. No one can occupy someone else's space even if they want to. I will stay in my place, Pamela in hers. No one will ever come into my life except you. But life cannot be sustained on love alone. Duty and responsibility are equally important. I must move forward, and so must you."

"I don't want to live anymore, Srimoyee."

"Listen carefully—make sure that little girl gets back her happy father. And what about your cigarette? Absolutely no smoking. Promise me."

"When you leave me, leave me completely, and don't worry about me needlessly. But since I can't ignore your wishes either, I promise—you'll get whatever you want."

"We won't stay in touch anymore. It will only make us more vulnerable and affect both our lives. We'll simply keep our memories of each other layered deep within our hearts. Let our relationship be defined by love, respect, and honour. If there's such a thing as rebirth, then Srimoyee and Arpan will be united. We will never part then. Now I must go. It's getting late. I have to go home."

Srimoyee got up, turned back and started walking briskly. She did not look back. She strode briskly toward the bus stop.

Arpan whispered to himself:

"Can you witness the passage of time?
Its chariot disappears every moment,
Awakening the pulse of the heart in the sky,
The stars wail in the wheel-crushed darkness.
O friend, that flowing time
Has entangled me in its net,
And swiftly carries me away on its chariot
Along the bold path of travel,
Far, far away from you.
It feels as if I have crossed
Countless deaths,
And today, atop the peak of a new dawn,
The restless speed of the chariot in the wind
Blows my old name away.
There is no way to return.
Even if I look from afar,

You will not be able to recognise me!
O friend, farewell!"

Suddenly, the mobile phone in Srimoyee's bag rang. It was Hari Kaka calling. "*Didibhai,* come quickly, mother isn't feeling well."

"What happened to mother?" Srimoyee's heart started pounding.

Mother and *Kakababu* were the only two people in this world whose presence she always felt in her life, and she believed they held her hands tightly in all walks of life. Srimoyee boarded the bus and tried to call Hari Kaka, but her phone's battery was low, and she could not contact Hari Kaka.

Chapter 17

As soon as Srimoyee came close to her house, she saw that a crowd had gathered outside. She hurried inside and found *Kakababu* sitting beside her mother's lifeless body, sobbing uncontrollably. Hari Kaka was trying to console Dr Basu.

The moment Dr Basu saw Srimoyee, he wailed and said, "*Boudi* is no more, *Didibhai*. She slipped in the bathroom while bathing and had a heart attack. I was in my chamber when Hari informed me. I left my work and rushed home, but by then, everything was over. *Boudi* didn't give us any time."

Srimoyee looked at her mother's face and collapsed onto the floor.

"*Didibhai*, be strong. I am here. You must complete your mother's last rites — you are her child. You dress her up for her journey. I had Hari bring everything we needed. We'll wait outside."

Srimoyee decked Lolita with garlands of tuberose, white sandal paste, tulsi leaves, and draped a fine *tussar* sari. Lolita's funeral was performed at Keoratala crematorium.

After the rituals were over and the school reopened after the Durga Puja break, Srimoyee went to school and submitted her resignation letter to Principal Sucheta Sanyal.

"Madam, I don't want to stay in this city anymore," she said.

The Principal asked her, "Are you trying to run away from the city or from your own life?"

"How can I run away from life? That isn't in my hands. But this city has drained me of everything, and I am exhausted. I don't want to stay here anymore."

"Have you decided where you'll go?"

"No, but somewhere far."

"You are the pride of our school — a responsible teacher. If you leave, it will be a great loss for us."

"I feel suffocated here, Madam. I can't stay. I want to live."

"Alright, take a few days to recover and then come back after a break."

"You already know everything about me, Ma'am. Sagarseni Mukherjee studies in this school. She is devoted to me and holds the key to my heart. Whenever she sees me, she clings to me. I want to go far away from all this."

"I understand your situation. Alright, listen... our school has an orphanage branch in Darjeeling — it's part of our institution. You can go there. They need a responsible principal. The current Principal is retiring this month. It's a hilly area that shelters orphaned children. Some of them are suffering from mental illness. Their parents ditch them and disappear. But many of these children are immensely talented. From what I know of you, you can nurture their talent and create a platform for them. If you take charge of the school, I will be immensely relieved. I know the work is difficult, but I am confident you will manage it well. You won't have any trouble there. There's a bungalow attached to the school — you can stay there. Staff will be available around the clock to assist you. However, the school doesn't have the facilities of a megacity school like Kolkata. Natural calamities like landslides occur frequently. Power cuts are frequent and can continue for days at a stretch. Water scarcity is another major issue. But despite all that, the serene environment will revive you."

At the very mention of Darjeeling, Srimoyee was startled. She asked the Principal, "What is the name of that home?"

"St. Mary's Child Home."

Srimoyee suddenly remembered seeing this very name on her vaccination card. It felt as if her place of birth was extending its arms to embrace and recall its lost daughter.

The Principal said, "Take your time and think. Give me your answer later. Life in the hills is beautiful, but it also comes with many challenges."

"I will have no problem, Ma'am. You can finalise it."

"Are you sure?"

"I want to take responsibility for that school, Madam."

"Today I am not speaking to you as your Principal, but as an elder sister. I've observed you for a long time — you are a person of great profundity. I bless you; good things will happen to you. This work will bring you mental peace. But our school will lose a dedicated and competent teacher. I'll prepare all your documents. Before that, let me say one more thing — I want to arrange a farewell programme for you on behalf of the school."

"No, Ma'am, please excuse me. I'm still going through my trauma and not yet ready for all this."

"Alright, but before you leave, I suggest you visit each class once, meet the teachers and students. You've given so many years to this school, and all the students are really very fond of you. I believe that for a teacher, the students are the most precious treasure. Children come to us to learn, they consider the school their second home, they spend the entire day with us — they are our family. That's why we always think about them. And I know you do too."

"This is exactly why my mind matches with yours, Ma'am — I care a lot. Even in my sleep, I see them in my dreams. I wonder which student needs a little more help to do better in exams, and how to make an inattentive child more focused on studies. These things occupy my thoughts. I want to do a lot for children — they are the ones who keep me alive."

"You'll have many opportunities to do just that in the school where you're going. And I know you'll succeed, because you have that talent in you."

"Alright, Ma'am, please prepare all the documents. Let me take one last walk through the school."

After meeting everyone, Srimoyee finally stood outside Sagarseni's classroom in the primary section. Her class teacher, Mrs Indira Bhattacharya, stood up from her chair when she saw Srimoyee and asked, "What brings you here, Madam?"

"Today is my last day in school, so I came to meet the students once."

Seeing Srimoyee, Sagarseni jumped up from her bench and said, "You won't leave me and go anywhere, Miss."

She advanced, hugged Srimoyee tightly, and broke down into tears. Immediately, all the students in the class chimed, "Don't leave us."

Srimoyee could not hold back her tears when she witnessed the love and adoration in the faces of those little children. This bolstered her confidence, and she felt she would surely pass this test of fate. Truly, children do not want much — only a little love. She remembered Lolita's words: 'The four walls of a household aren't meant for you, Sri— a bigger world beckons you…' She remembered that doing something for little orphaned children and bringing changes in their lives is like serving God; not everyone gets this opportunity.

Wiping her tears, freeing herself gently from Sagarseni's hands, Srimoyee said, "Stay well. Study hard. You must grow up to be a good human being."

Then, looking at the rest of the class, she smiled softly and said, "I'm telling you all — study with dedication, strengthen the ground beneath your feet, become established in life. If you all build yourselves up, our country will grow because of you. Remember, work hard and achieve great results. Make your parents and country proud."

After returning home from school, Srimoyee packed her bags. Hari Kaka and *Kakababu* were standing outside her room.

"May we come in?" they asked.

Srimoyee said, "*Kakababu,* why are you seeking my permission? Please come in."

Hari Kaka said, "Both of our bags are packed already."

"Where are you both going?" she asked.

Dr. Basu replied, "Why? With you, of course! I've had enough of chambers and nursing homes. I don't enjoy that anymore. The moment I heard you were leaving, my heart leapt. It's been many years since I last went to the hills. So, I handed over the responsibility of the nursing home to Mr Ronojoy Chakraborty. But I'll visit from time to time — I have to. I'll come occasionally to check on things. I told Hari to stay here and take care of the house, but he won't leave me alone. So, Hari is coming with us too."

"But I've already bought a ticket, *Kakababu*."

"Cancel that ticket — I've already bought three tickets together," said Dr Basu, placing his hand on her head. "How could you think, my child, that I would let you go alone? I haven't done much free medical service lately, so I thought — since you are going for such a noble cause, I too should join in the noble programme and earn a little merit. After a lifetime of running around, I don't feel like staying alone anymore at this age, *Didibhai*. Besides, what's the point of accumulating so much wealth and property? Will that help me pay for my journey to heaven? So, I've decided to go to the hills and breathe some fresh air."

Hari Kaka said, "That's it — everything is settled. I can't stay here alone without you and *Babu*. So, I have packed my bags as well. After tonight, we wake up tomorrow to a new land, with new challenges and loads of fun. So off we go to join our mission — Darjeeling's St. Mary's Child Home."